A Section 31 Novel
Book 1

By T. R. Bryan

UNDERBELLY

The Return of Jax Nandi

ISBN: 9781720051077

Give feedback on the book at:

trbryan601@gmail.com

Author's Note

For those of you who are unfamiliar with the Star Trek universe may I recommend two websites that should be of great value to you? The first website displays a star map of the Alpha and Beta Quadrants. This book takes place entirely in the Beta Quadrant close to the Romulan Neutral Zone.
The second website includes pictures and brief summaries of the different species named in this book.

For Alpha and Beta Quadrant Star Chart you can Google *'star trek star charts'*.

For Alpha and Beta Quadrant Species you can Google *'star trek species memory alpha'*.

I hope this helps.

T. R. Bryan

"*Interesting, isn't it? The Federation claims to abhor Section 31's tactics, but when they need the dirty work done, they look the other way. It's a tidy little arrangement, wouldn't you say?*"

Odo, 2375 ("The Dogs of War")

Prologue

1 year ago.

Omicron IV is the outermost planet orbiting a Type 'G' white dwarf star in space claimed by the United Federation of Planets. This particular star system is in close proximity to the Neutral Zone set up between the Romulan Star Empire and the Federation over a century ago.

100 million years ago Omicron IV's surface was almost entirely water. 75 million years of seismic and volcanic upheavals and mantel shifting resulted in the formation of a large single continent about the size of Europe and Asia combined. The next 10 million years resulted in massive amounts of rain and flooding which carved the volcanic rock into patterns like a jigsaw puzzle. Thousands of varying sized canyons and tunnels stretching for hundreds of kilometers have been formed. Many are visible from space. Others, not visible but are there none the less. Smaller fractures on the earth can hide massive canyons. Attempts to survey the canyon system have been unsuccessful because the composition of the rocks make it difficult for sensors to penetrate.

This rugged canyon-like terrain takes up approximately 60% of the landmass mostly to the north of the continent. The remaining 40% is covered by rolling hills fertile plains, small lakes and a large river with hundreds of tributaries that flows out of the canyonlands in the north and empties into the ocean to the south of the continent.

During the late spring rainy season nutrients wash down from the eroding canyons flooding large areas of land. In spite of the fertility of the soil and abundance of water, flora and fauna are limited. This is because the planet is in its early stages of evolution and as such only mosses lichens exist. Millennia from now, they will be replaced by plants and trees but for now, the planet is a work in progress.

Class 'L' planets like Omicron IV are normally allowed to evolve on their own but because it had been outside of the territorial boundaries established by the United Federation of Planets, terra farmers began planting forests and grasslands on the planet. This started taking place around seventy-five years ago. Twenty years later flowers and bees were introduced. Seed-eating birds came next. Five years after that came grazing animals and predators. After another five years of letting nature take its course, the terra farmers moved in. They have been there ever since.

Because of the remoteness of the planet, the population has never been large but it has managed to remain fairly constant over the years, living mostly off the land and mostly foregoing modern conveniences.

The Tal Shiar, the Romulan Star Empire's Intelligence Agency, has been monitoring the progress on Omicron IV since the first terra farmers arrived. They filed several protests with the Federation claiming that the planet would be used as a staging area for an invasion or some covert plot. The Federation assured them that this was not the case and they were more than welcome to monitor the planet as long as it was done within Romulan space. After years of monitoring the planet, the Romulans finally accepted the fact that Omicron IV was not an immediate threat. However, monitoring still continues but to a lesser degree.

The closest habitable planet to Omicron IV is located in the Tukaris star system claimed by the Romulan Star Empire. Of the three planets orbiting the white dwarf star only the middle planet, Tukaris II would be deemed fit for habitation. The temperatures on the planet are similar to Earth's before a planetary weather grid was installed with winters reaching as low as -50 degrees Celsius at the poles and over 45 degrees Celsius at the equator. With a weather grid more of the planet would be habitable but because of its remoteness and the makeup of its current occupants the Romulan government chooses to ignore it.

The planet's inhabitants are Romulans who called themselves the Believers. The Believers, who consider themselves as "True

Romulans", were founded almost eighty years ago. A noted archeologist named Mordock Hartume and his team unearthed tablets written in a language that predated any known Romulan language while working at ruins of an early Romulan civilization believed to be 32,000 years old in the D'Nev Desert on Romulus. Although the civilization predates other known Romulan societies, there appears to be no known correlation between it and the others.

Over the next eighteen months, Dr. Hartume and his team worked tirelessly to decipher the text. During this time Dr. Hartume became more and more entranced with the beauty and sophistication of the language and the meaning of the text. So much so that team members expressed their concern that he was losing his scientific objectivity. Dr. Hartume scoffed at their concerns and continued his work.

What the text revealed was a philosophy outlining how a true believer should conduct his life. The philosophy was called *"The Way."* Reading *"The Way"* in modern-day Romulan revealed a philosophy that while impressive had little to do with the realities of current day Romulan life. However, reading *"The Way"* in the ancient language was intoxicating. It was as if the language could control your emotions.

Dr. Hartume and some of his team embraced the latter while the remainder of his team thought of it as a rare archeological find of historical significance and nothing more. These conflicting views caused a rift between team members that could not be closed. When it became time to publish his findings Dr. Hartume insisted that his interpretation of the tablets and philosophy be used. Others disagreed. A compromise was made where both views would be presented for review.

Four months later Dr. Hartume presented his findings to the Romulan Antiquities Council for review. Much to his dismay, the Council rejected his conclusion and accepted the conclusion of his dissenters. One Council member noted that for all they knew, strict adherence to *The Way* could have led to the downfall of this civilization. They recommended that more research be done before the Antiquities Council would consider his findings for review.

Distraught, Dr. Hartume resigned his membership in the Antiquities Council and abandoned his research in the desert. He and his associates were convinced that *The Way* was the future and it needed to be taught to every Romulan in order to fulfill their lives. They decided to call themselves the Believers and they aggressively set out to bring *The Way* to all of Romulus.

It didn't take long for Romulan officials to take notice of the Believers. Complaints poured in all over the planet. So much so that many of the leaders were arrested and jailed. However, Dr. Hartume along with other leaders and followers were pre-warned and acquired passage on a starship that took them to Tukaris II. There were about two hundred Believers who made the journey.

With the departure of Dr. Hartume from Romulus, the ranks of the Believers dwindled and died. As a result, the jailed adherents were freed and given the opportunity to settle on Tukaris II with Dr. Hartume provided that they not return to Romulus. The Empire would provide all Believers with provisions for one year along with tools to allow them to live off the land. Two hundred and fifty Believers took the offer and left Romulus.

Little did the Empire know that in addition to provisions and personal items, the Believers smuggled a large, very powerful radio transmitter on the ship with them. If they couldn't spread *The Way* in person on Romulus, they would transmit it throughout the Galaxy.

Within days after arriving at Tukaris II, the transmitter was up and running giving the galaxy an uninterrupted stream of *The Way*. The Empire immediately blocked the transmission frequencies and within days a ship was dispatched to Tukaris II to surround the planet with satellites which would block all incoming and outgoing transmissions. The satellites also transmitted a quarantine message for ships nearing the planet.

The Empire would periodically send a ship to maintain the satellites and monitor the planet's inhabitants. After 20 years it was determined that only the quarantine message would continue. At 25 years the satellites orbits were beginning to decay and fall into the atmosphere. It was decided that the Believers were no longer a threat and no more resources would be allocated to monitor them. For the last 55 years, the planet has been quiet.

Then, two days ago, an emergency distress beacon was activated.

The Romulan ship T'Nitzi was a Talon Class vessel with a crew complement of 28. Talon Class ships are lightly armed vessels known for their speed and maneuverability. A typical Talon Class vessel has a forward firing disruptor array plus two forward and one aft torpedo bays. They normally only carry eight photon torpedoes which are to be used for defensive purposes.

The T'Nitzi is equipped with a highly sophisticated sensor array which the ship had used to monitor the Neutral Zone with the United Federation of Planets for the last three months. They had spent the last three days monitoring transmissions to and from Omicron IV without incident and were headed home when the Romulan High Command ordered them to divert to the Tukaris system, four days out of their way, to determine why the distress beacon was activated.

"Commander, we've reached the Tukaris system and are dropping out of warp... and Commander, I'm picking up a quarantine message from the second planet" helmsman Jiket informed Cmdr. Bakil who was sitting in his ready room.

"Inform me when we are orbiting Tukaris II", responded the Commander. "Also, scan for other vessels in the star system and use long-range scanners to scan for ships in this sector."

"Understood Commander."

"Communications officer? Inform Central Command that we've reached our destination?"

"Aye, Commander."

Cmdr. Bakil was a 53-year veteran of the Romulan military. He had been a starship Commander for 18 years, the last five as Commander of the T'Nitzi. He was awarded several commendations during the Dominion War for bravery and dedication.

His outward appearance could best be described as "average." Average looks; average height; average weight. Nothing outstanding. Then as you talked to him you realized why he commands a starship. He had a quick mind, exceptional tactical skills, and a sharp wit. He values his crew and they would do anything for him.

Sometimes a quick wit can get you in trouble as Cmdr. Bakil found out when he once made an observation in a joking manner about how bureaucratic dealings between the regular military and the Tal Shiar can sometimes be. Unfortunately, the "joke" made its way to the Tal Shiar and his promising career came to an abrupt halt. Cmdr. Bakil went from a prospective Warbird Commander to commanding a ship that would fit into a Warbird's cargo bay. In spite of the rebuke, Cmdr. Bakil has continued to serve the Empire to the best of his abilities.

With him in his ready room were First Officer Sub-Commander Dimiuth, Second Officer and Science Officer Sub-commander Mokath, head of security Centurion Sokun and ship's medical officer Dr. Romix. Dr. Romix was more of a general practitioner than a surgeon. Because the T'Nitzi had a small crew, the Empire didn't see the need for using a skilled surgeon. If any problems arose that were beyond Dr. Romix's abilities the patient was to be placed in one of the four stasis chambers on the ship and tended to when a skilled surgeon was available.

"Gentlemen, it should be a several minutes before we receive a response back from Central Command as to why we were sent to this god-forsaken part of the galaxy", said Cmdr. Bakil. "I'm just as much in the dark as you on this matter. The only thing I do know is that quarantine message was put there decades ago. Why? I don't really know."

"Commander", responded Centurion Sokun. "I must be honest. I have never heard of the Tukaris system before."

"I've seen it on star charts and knew it has three planets but I've seen nothing to indicate that any of the planets were habitable", responded Sub-Cmdr. Mokath. "I hope this isn't one of those missions where Central Command tells us to forget everything we've seen? I'd like to truthfully explain to my wife why I have to be away from home another two weeks or more."

"I've heard things about Tukaris II years ago by some of the older crewmen who claimed to have visited the planet", said Cmdr. Bakil. "Of course, they are only rumors and you can't trust the reliability of the information when it's coming from someone full of Romulan ale."

Everyone laughed at this.

"Anyhow, one rumor said it was a secret testing base. I kind of discount this because the person who said it couldn't keep a secret if his mouth was welded shut."

More laughter.

"The other rumor was that the planet was used as a penal colony. Hardened criminals and enemies of the state are sent there to die. This would be a little more plausible if the planet was patrolled by a Warbird to prevent criminals from escaping. I'm sure that quarantine message wouldn't prevent anyone from coming to or leaving the planet." The Commander continued, "I guess we'll find out when Central Command contacts us. Any more questions?"

"Yes, Commander" replied Sub-Cmdr. Dimiuth. "I..."

"Commander, this is the bridge. Priority message from Central Command."

"Patch it through to my ready room" replied Cmdr. Bakil. "Sorry, Dimiuth. Hold that question for later."

Seconds later the viewscreen brightened and the figure of Vice-Admiral Kemor appeared. Adm. Kemor was a distinguished man in his early hundreds. He had salt and pepper hair common for a man of his age and the haggard face of a man who had spent decades making decisions that affected the health and safety of the Empire.

Adm. Kemor wasted no time in asking "Commander, first and foremost, are there any Tal Shiar agents on your ship?"

"No Admiral, there aren't" replied Bakil.

"Good, I can speak freely... What's your current status?"

"We're just starting to orbit the second planet. We will make a sweep of the planet and adjust our orbit based on what we find' said Cmdr. Bakil. "By the way Admiral, what are we looking for?"

"Since ordering you there, I've been trying to get information about the planet and its occupants from the Tal Shiar," said the Admiral. Then he said sarcastically "You don't know how much I enjoy dealing with them on a regular basis. "

"From what the Tal Shiar was willing to contribute, Tukaris II has been occupied by a bunch of Romulan malcontents who call themselves the Believers. The Tal Shiar wouldn't go into why they considered them malcontents and I didn't ask." The Admiral went on, "They've been on Tukaris II for the last 75 years. For the first twenty-five years or so the Tal Shiar would monitor them to see what kind of technological advances they were making. If they were advancing too rapidly, the Tal Shiar would consider them a threat and deal with them."

"During that time the Believers appeared to have no interest in technology and seemed quite content with living off the land. Their only interest outside the planet was broadcasting messages into space hoping someone would hear them. The Tal Shiar remedied this by surrounding the planet with satellites that would block all incoming and outgoing communications. Somewhere around the 20th year, all outbound transmissions had stopped. At 25 years, it was decided to shut down the satellites except for a few that issued quarantine messages that kept outsiders away from the planet."

The Admiral went on "There were approximately 450 Believers that settled there and by the end of the Tal Shiar's monitoring there were around eight hundred. The Tal Shiar estimates there would be around 1,900 to 3,000 Believers now depending on how well they've adapted."

"Four days ago an automated emergency broadcast was sent from the planet and ran for about six hours. We don't know whether it was a legitimate call for help or a malfunction of an aging system."

"Your orders are to scan the planet for life. If there is a healthy population, do nothing. Just perform a census and report your findings back to me. "If the population is low, try to determine the cause. It could be the climate, plague or an enemy attack. Whatever it is find the cause without coming into direct contact with them."

"Commander, keep in mind that the Tal Shiar is deeply involved. Do your job, report back and forget about everything you've seen."

Why did I know this was going to happen thought sub-Commander Mokath?

Cmdr. Bakil asked, "Admiral if the Tal Shiar is involved, why are we here?"

"Because your ship was the closest. You just happened to be in the wrong place at the wrong time" replied the Admiral. "Any more questions?"

"Yes, Admiral," said Cmdr. Bakil already knowing what the answer would be. "What were the Believers broadcasting?"

The Admiral had a glum look on his face. "I made the mistake and asked the same thing. I was told that it was none of my concern."

"Understood, Admiral."

"Kemor out." And the screen went blank.

Cmdr. Bakil turned away from his viewscreen and looked directly at his officers. "Okay, you heard the admiral. Let get this done."

With that, the officers stood, exited the ready room and entered the bridge. The T'Nitzi had just arrived at Tukaris II and was beginning to orbit the planet.

"Helmsman, anchor us above the largest settlement on the planet," said the Commander.

"Aye Commander."

A few minutes later Helmsman Jiket said "Commander, there appear to be four settlements of various sizes, all in the same hemisphere. We're directly above what appears to be the largest settlement. From here it looks like it could house 800 people or so."

"Mister Mokath, what are sensors picking up?"

"Nothing Commander... Let me rephrase that. Sensors are not picking up any movement whatsoever in the settlement. No people. No animals. I am picking up some small bird-like animals but not very many. This planet is nothing but dense forest, rocks and numerous small lakes. Sensors are having a hard time cutting through the forest, so it's hard to tell what's under the tree canopy" was Mr. Mokath's response.

"That's not exactly what I was hoping you would say, Mister," said the Commander. "Mister Mokath, what about non-moving life forms? I mean, can you identify bodies?"

"Scanning now Commander". After a few moments of checking and rechecking Mr. Mokath said: "Commander, there appear to be bodies, maybe the settlers but I can't be sure."

"What do you mean you can't be sure" replied the Commander.

"Well, most of the bodies don't look right. Something's missing. Should we beam one aboard and have Doctor Romix examine it?"

"Absolutely not" Cmdr. Bakil forcefully. "We have no idea whether this was caused by civil war or plague. I'm not endangering the ship's crew until we know what's going on. We'll scan the other settlements for life. If none exist, we'll hand this over to the Tal Shiar and let them put their crew at risk... Helmsman, take us to another settlement."

The T'Nitzi scanned the next two settlements both having the same results, dead Romulan bodies and livestock that appeared to be mutilated. The fourth settlement had fewer dwellings than the first three but they were spread out over a larger area.

"Nothing so far, Commander," said Sub-Cmdr. Mokath. "I don't... Wait. I'm picking up something in what appears to be a barn just north of the settlement... It appears to be Romulan... the life signs look weak but stable. It looks like a male. Commander, should we beam him aboard?"

"No. Not until we talk to Central Command" said the Commander. "Communications, contact Admiral Kemor and patch it into my ready room. Dimiuth, Mokath, you're with me." Tapping his communicator, Cmdr. Bakil began to speak "Doctor Romix please report to my ready room."

Minutes later, Adm. Kemor's image appeared on the viewscreen. "Status, Commander."

"Admiral, all but one of the inhabitants are dead. We haven't beamed the male survivor up yet because we're not sure how everyone died. Should we send an away team to the surface? We'll take all the precautions."

"No" replied the admiral. "The Tal Shiar doesn't want you down there. As for the survivor, the Tal Shiar probably won't want you talking to him either. Is there any way to bring him on board without endangering the ship?"

"Well," Cmdr. Bakil hesitated. "We could beam him directly into a stasis chamber. We could keep him in hibernation until we return home" replied the commander.

"I think the Tal Shiar would find your plan acceptable Commander." The admiral continued "How many stasis chambers are aboard your ship, Commander?"

"Four, sir."

"It would probably be a good idea to place some of the casualties into stasis and let the Tal Shiar perform the autopsies," said the admiral.

"Understood, sir."

"Oh, one more thing Commander. I'm changing your orders" said the admiral. "You will remain at Tukaris II until the Tal Shiar relieves you. A Warbird is being sent today."

"Sir, couldn't we meet the Warbird halfway? We've been out here a long time?"

"No. If the planet has been attacked, whoever did it might return? If they do, we need you to be there."

"Understood, Admiral" replied Cmdr. Bakil. "When can we expect the Tal Shiar to arrive?"

"At least five days" replied the admiral. "Sorry Commander. This just isn't your day. We'll extend your leave time when you return. In the meantime, gather as much information as you can about the planet. Also, see if you can find any warp signatures... Kemor out."

"Oh, great" replied Sub-Cmdr. Mokath. "My wife is going to love this."

"Just tell her that 'Duty Calls' and leave it at that," said the commander. "That's what I always do when I'm delayed."

"Does it work?"

"No. Not really."

Cmdr. Bakil looked over at Dr. Romix. "Please supervise the transfer of the survivor?"

Five days after the lone survivor and three bodies were beamed aboard the T'Nitzi and put into stasis, the Romulan Warbird, *M'Elshazhak*, arrived at Tukaris II and moved into a matching orbit with T'Nitzi. Seeing both starships together reminded you of a wren next to an eagle.

The *M'Elshazhak* was a D'deridex class starship, over five hundred meters in length, armed with enough firepower to destroy a small moon. The ship had a crew of 950 which included 300 battle-tested Reman troops, just in case they were needed.

The M'Elshazhak was commanded by Commander Venesa. Cmdr. Venesa was in her early 70's and had been with the Tal Shiar since she graduated from the military academy. She stood almost six feet high and was solidly built, making her a very imposing figure. She was a more than capable commander who had seen her share of action during the Dominion War.

"Commander, the M'Elshazhak is hailing us," said Lt. Jolar, the T'Nitzi's communication officer.

"Put it on the viewscreen, Centurion," said Cmdr. Bakil from his Commander's chair on the bridge. The screen lit up and the image of Commander Venesa appeared.

"Commander Venesa, I see you made good time getting here."

"Commander Bakil, yes, we pushed the ship as hard as we could to get here. Your initial report of the situation was indeed unusual. It definitely warranted the Tal Shiar's inclusion... What have you discovered so far?"

"As you are aware, we were not allowed to send a team to the planet. We were able to gather quite a bit of information over the past five days. What we can tell you is that it was definitely an attack" said Cmdr. Bakil. "There are traces of disruptor fire at all four sites."

"Is there any reason to suspect the Federation?"

"No. Things have been quiet along the Neutral Zone. No unusual ship movements, no chatter whatsoever" said Cmdr. Bakil. "This definitely wasn't anything the Federation did and it doesn't look like anything the Federation would do."

He continued. "We also detected a warp signature. It was faint but we could tell it wasn't a Federation ship. And it was heading away from the Neutral Zone and into uncharted space."

"We have both the survivor and three bodies in stasis. We'll beam them over shortly. The survivor is a young male. He appears a bit malnourished but in good health. The bodies? Well, that's another story."

"What do you mean" asked Cmdr. Venesa?

"Well, all three victims appear to have had their chest cavities sliced open. For what reason and with what, we don't know."

"Have you found any large lifeforms on the planet that may be responsible for this?"

"No, not one" replied Cmdr. Bakil. "There have been smaller scavengers around the settlements but nothing large enough to rip through Romulan flesh like that. It looks like your ship's surgeon is going to be kept busy on this. We can begin the transfer at any..."

"Commander, long-range sensors have picked up ships coming from the direction of the warp signature," said Sub-commander Mokath interrupting the conversation.

Commander Venesa immediately looked to her left and said "Centurion, can you confirm?" Seconds later, a voice to his left said "Confirmed sir. There appear to be three ships headed our way. One is our size. The other two are much smaller."

Cmdr. Venesa turned her head back to the viewscreen and looked into Cmdr. Bakil's eyes. "Commander, please begin the transfer. We'll cloak and wait for our visitors to arrive."

"Commander, this is not a fighting vessel. I can probably damage the smaller ships but that's only if I can hit them before they raise their shields."

"Understood, Commander," said Cmdr. Venesa. "If I can take out the bigger ship before its shields raise. We should have no problem with the smaller ones."

"Understood."

The transfer completed and both ships immediately cloaked. Cmdr. Bakil scanned the bridge, looking at all of his officers. Then he turned his head back at Sub-Cmdr. Mokath. "Sub-Commander? How soon before they arrive?"

"A little over five hours, sir."

Cmdr. Bakil tapped his communicator. "This is the Commander. In five hours we will engage an unknown enemy who has attacked and slaughtered unarmed civilians. I expect nothing but your best. Bakil out." Cmdr. Bakil looked over to his friend Sub-Cmdr. Dimiuth: "And now, we wait."

He then looked back into the viewscreen at the approaching ships and thought to himself *Duty Calls*.

PART ONE

Chapter 1

Current Day.
The Earth year is 2381. Six years have passed since the end of the Dominion War and the devastation caused by that conflict was still being felt. In the war's two-year timespan over one billion lives were taken. The Cardassian Union alone lost over 900 million of its citizens. Over eighty percent of its military was also destroyed leaving most of its territory unprotected.

The great irony of war is that you spend it trying to defeat your enemy's army to win and after you've won you spend more time and resources trying to rebuild that army so yours can go home. This was true in this war because the Federation spent five years and scores of starships trying to maintain the peace while the Cardassians rebuilt a defense force that was capable of patrolling inside their borders.

This was no easy feat because the Federation had over 91 million casualties itself. None the less, they agreed to stay and protect them until the Cardassian Union could protect themselves.

The Klingon Empire had agreed to provide security but that didn't last long. The Klingons are warriors and not policemen and only helped for one year. In reality, providing security for one year exceeded the expectations the Federation had for the Klingons.

As for the Romulan Star Empire, the relationship between them and the Federation began as a period of cooperation and friendship but as the years went by the communication between the two powers began to wane. Finally, one year ago all communications stopped. Attempts were made to reestablish communications to no avail. Starfleet Security, the Federation's intelligence organization, could only attribute it to some internal strife, which was not unusual for Romulan politics and recommended that the Federation wait until the Romulans decided it was time to reemerge.

Since the end of the war, the Federation began a massive rebuilding of Starfleet. Hundreds of ships and hundreds of thousands of military personnel had died during that conflict and the effort to replace them was at full swing. Ships were built. Captains and crews were assigned. Nothing like this had ever happened before in Starfleet's history.

Fourteen months ago a human female named Aisha Aziz was promoted to captain. This would normally be nothing out the ordinary but in her case, she was far from being ordinary for three reasons. First, she was promoted to captain just before her thirtieth birthday, something that had only been accomplished four times in the history of Starfleet.

Second, she was promoted to captain in less than six years, a feat only accomplished by one other Starfleet officer.

And third, she graduated in the bottom third of her class, something that usually disqualified a Starfleet officer from ever achieving the rank of Commander let alone Captain.

Capt. Aziz is the current commanding officer of the *USS Fermi*, Registry number NCC-71549. The *Fermi* is an Intrepid Class starship that was built in the Earth year 2372, a year after its sister ship the *USS* Voyager. Unlike the Voyager, the *Fermi* was originally designed specifically for scientific exploration and as such more interior space was allocated for science labs and holodecks. The original plans were that it would have fewer offensive capabilities than the Voyager but that changed when rifts between the Federation and the Klingon Empire started to appear.

The *Fermi* saw action during the Dominion War and was a member of the armada that defeated the Dominion' Fleet at Cardassia Prime.

The *Fermi* has a crew complement of 225 which includes 125 support officers and crewmen and 100 scientists of various disciplines. Besides Capt. Aziz, the command staff consists of First Officer Cmdr. Roy Montgomery, a human; Second Officer Cmdr. Gintok, a Benzite; Chief Science Officer Lt. Cmdr. Anauk, a Vulcan;

Chief Engineer Lt. Cmdr. Adele Klein, a human; Chief Security Officer Lt. Tatiana 'Anna' Shushunova-Nandi, a human and Ship's Surgeon Dr. Sornax, a Denobulan. All officers except for Lt. Shushunova-Nandi, who joined the crew nine months ago, were members of the crew before Capt. Aziz took command.

Chapter 2

The sun in the Ostara System which is located in the Omicron Sector eighteen light years from the Romulan Neutral Zone was beginning to nova. For several billion years it was a yellow dwarf star similar in size and mass to the one Earth orbits. Then a few million years ago nitrogen within the star began to deplete raising its temperature which caused the sun to expand into the red giant it is today.

Federation scientists believed that the core of the sun would begin to collapse in the next two to three months resulting in the surface of the sun burning brighter until it began to dim several months after that.

The *Fermi* has been in orbiting the sun for the last two weeks. For the scientists, it has been a flurry of activity making sure the sensors are perfectly calibrated and strategically placed in order to study every hiccup the sun made. Even though the ship's sensors were monitoring every movement, the scientists on board were foregoing sleep determined to 'be there' if something unexpected happens. Novae happen about once every fifty years in the galaxy and for a scientist, this is a once in a lifetime experience.

For the officers and support crew of the *Fermi*, the last two weeks have been anything but exciting. The command staff got to go to daily meetings where they hear about how the star is expanding at 100 meters per day and how the only remaining planet's surface temperature is increasing a quarter degree Celsius every eighteen hours and other scientific tidbits that they either didn't take at the Academy or struggled through hoping they would never be asked about it again. The common crewman, on the other hand, would occasionally look out one of the ship's many portholes and see a sun that pretty much looked the same as it did when they first arrived two weeks earlier.

The best way to describe the atmosphere on the *Fermi* is to quote Dickens: *It was the best of times. It was the worst of times.*

As the week wore on the number of ships arriving had doubled with long-ranged sensors showing more ships on their way. This was the astrological event of the decade and no one wanted to miss it.

By the middle of the third week two more Federation science ships had arrived, the *USS Tyson*, captained by Capt. Arch Stanton and *USS Sagan* captained by Capt. Fawn Liebowitz. Their mission was the same as the *Fermi*, to observe but things usually aren't that simple.

The universe is infinite but you can only get so many ships observing one sun at the same time. It sounds ridiculous but it was true. As the number of ships in the area increased, so did their mission. They were now part-time traffic cops and occasional referees when disputes arose. It was amazing to see so many species of intelligent beings in one place reverting back to their ancient primitive instincts when another science ship encroached on what they perceived as 'their' best view of the sun. To the many science vessels there, it was no longer just an observation. It was a competition.

This was definitely a time when Capt. Aziz' diplomatic skills were used to their full extent as she and the other two starship captains worked tirelessly to prevent hostilities from breaking out between the many alien species.

Things were no longer boring.

Chapter 3

Near the end of the fourth week Adm. Lydia Merino, the Omicron Sector's commanding officer, held a briefing with the senior officers of the three science ships via subspace. The officers were told that the Planetary Security Agency on Toriga IV had received intelligence that the Talesian Brotherhood, a notorious band of pirates that had plagued the surrounding sectors for the last two decades, was planning a raid on their planet within the next ninety-six hours. The *USS Georgetown* was being dispatched to the area in the hope that it could capture and/or destroy some of the Brotherhood's ships and crews. The captains were also told that they should be ready to assist in the defense of Toriga IV if needed.

Toriga IV is a warp-capable society that was not yet a member of the Federation. They had a small but capable military but their defenses surrounding the planet were woefully inadequate. The Federation had offered to upgrade their planetary defenses as well as leave a garrison of 100 Starfleet Security personnel to reinforce the Torigan military. The Torigan government considered the offer but declined because the threat from the Talesian Brotherhood, if credible, was immediate and upgrading the planet's defenses would take months. The Torigans also did not like the idea of an alien army occupying their planet for an extended period.

A compromise was agreed upon in which a small Federation security contingent would be allowed on the planet for the extent of the threat and then removed. It was also decided that the *Georgetown* would not go to the planet but stay within striking distance of it so the Brotherhood would not know that their plans had been discovered.

Because the *Georgetown* would not be in position for another 36 hours, Adm. Merino ordered each captain to select ten security members from each ship and take three shuttles to

Toriga IV where they would support the military. The thirty-man contingent would include the most qualified security officer and two chief petty officers. The three captains would decide who was most qualified.

Capt. Aziz expressed her concerns about the mission and volunteered her ship to assist the *Georgetown*. Her concerns and request were noted and denied because the Brotherhood usually made their raids with a maximum of six ships and the *Georgetown* was larger and had more firepower than the three science ships combined. Adm. Merino noted that if there was any reason to think that the tactics normally used by the Brotherhood had changed, all three ships would be deployed until other ships in the sector were available to relieve them.

After the admiral signed off, the three captains discussed who would lead the mission. Lt. Shushunova-Nandi of the *Fermi* was picked for the mission because she had the most experience. One chief would be picked from *Tyson* and *Sagan* to complete the command team. The selected teams would assemble in two hours and leave for their seventeen-hour trip to Toriga IV at Warp 5.

Lt. Tatiana 'Ana' Shushunova-Nandi had been a Starfleet Security officer ever since she graduated from Starfleet Academy eighteen years ago. During that time she had served at two Starbases and on four different starships. She and her husband transferred to the *Fermi* nine months ago where she was given her first command position as the ship's Head of Security. If she proved herself, getting promoted to Lt. Cmdr. would not be out of the question.

The 40-year-old was 5’11” tall and had a thin but well-muscled frame, weighing 160 lbs., with short red hair and a milk-white complexion.

Her life had seemed to change after she met her husband Jackson Nandi six years ago. When she met him she knew he was the person she would marry. At first, he didn’t take her seriously because he and her father were the same age. *“Marry someone your own age. You won’t like changing my diapers twenty years from now”* he would tell her. In spite of that, she continued to pursue him and finally, he realized she was serious and the rest was history. They've been happily married for the last five years.

Well, pretty much happily married. The only thing that has annoyed her was that she had yet to win the love and affection of her husband's 40-pound Bajoran Cat, Crewman Kaso. The really odd thing about it was that as far as anyone knew, Crewman Kaso was the only Bajoran Cat that had ever been domesticated. They were usually solitary animals that didn't do well in confined spaces like zoos but this one had made herself at home in their small apartment and thought she owned the place.

The cat was like putty in her husband's hands but when Ana said anything to it, all she got in return were hisses and flashing fangs. Fortunately, the cat had never tried to scratch or bite her. It did, however, bare its two-inch razor-sharp claws once when she had said something that the cat must have sensed was an insult. *It's like living with a teen-aged daughter who thinks your household rules are too strict*, she thought. After that, she just made the assumption that she was actually a teenager and treated her as such, like talking to her calmly and their relationship improved.

What she found most strange was that the cat seemed to understand everything that her husband said to her and would make cat-like noises back to him as if it were replying back to him. At times she would pay attention to what he was telling it and observe the cat's responses. She realized that it was a lot more than just body language and emotion the cat was picking up.

An hour after the briefing Lt. Shushunova-Nandi was in her apartment preparing for her trip to Toriga IV when her husband Jackson entered.

Lt. Jackson Mandela 'Jax' Nandi was without a doubt the best engineer on the *Fermi*. Some would argue he was one of the best engineers in Starfleet and could easily have been the Chief Engineer on any starship he chose. He was the top engineer in his graduating class, fifth cadet overall, at Starfleet Academy forty-five years ago. But in spite of his obvious talents, he showed no interest in being promoted and taking on the responsibilities of a leadership role but preferred to spend his career going from starship to starship working on different projects and occasionally being sent to Starfleet to work on special projects, which for some unknown reason were always vaguely documented in his personnel record.

He was the youngest child of Mpilo Nandi and Vanessa Wadsworth-Nandi. His mother's lineage dated back to pre-Victorian England where it was traditional for the men of her family to join the military. His father's lineage dated back to the formation of the Zulu Empire in South Africa. Coincidently or ironically, depending on your point of view, the Nandi and Wadsworth families met once before. It was in 1879 at the Battle of Isandlwana in South Africa when an army of Zulu warriors armed with only spears and hide shields defeated a smaller but technologically superior army of the British Empire. Jax had ancestors fighting on both sides but only one survived.

Lt. Nandi's career had indeed been long. He had celebrated his 67th birthday two months ago and to a casual observer, he looked like he was in his early forties. He was 6' tall and weighed 185 lbs. and had probably been that weight for the last 40 years. His complexion leaned more toward his mother's and he had started keeping his hair trimmed short since it began thinning around the time that he turned sixty. To put it simply, he was a superb physical specimen.

Jax was known to have a rather strange sense of humor and would recite quotes from late-20th and early-21st-century movies and literature when he couldn't find an answer or resolve a problem.

In the Federation pecking order, he was the trailing spouse and when Ana was transferred, he came along for the ride.

"What in the wide, wide world of sports is going on here," asked Jax with a smile? As he spoke Crewman Kaso came out of the bedroom and purred when she saw him. He turned toward it. "Crewman, have you treated your ranking lieutenant with the respect she deserves?" The cat let out a low growl.

He walked over to Ana and gave her a small peck on the lips. "Now, Lieutenant, back to you."

Ana smiled at her husband. "Oh, Jax. A security team I'm leading is being sent to Toriga IV to provide technical support to their military."

Jax' smile faded as he stepped back from her and asked "Technical support? As in shooting and fighting?"

Ana's smile faded "Most likely. There is intelligence that indicates that the Talesian Brotherhood may attempt a raid on the planet. I'll be leading a team of thirty security personnel on shuttles. We'll be leaving in an hour."

"Talesian Brotherhood? Shuttles? Leaving in an hour? When did all this happen?"

"Oh, an hour ago. It came as a surprise to me, too."

"Don't they have other, larger starships with lots of people on them?"

"They do but we're much closer and there's no guarantee that the Brotherhood will actually attack."

Jax' expression turned to one of eagerness. "Well in that case, how about I tag along with you?"

Ana laughed. "Seriously, Jax. When were you in an actual combat situation?"

"Well, it's been a few years but fighting bad hombres is kind of like riding a bicycle. Once you learn it, it's easy to start up again."

Ana laughed and then said sternly "Jax. You aren't qualified for this mission. If you were to get hurt, I could never forgive myself."

"I'm not concerned about me. I'm concerned about you... There's something about this that just isn't right."

Ana shook her head. "I will agree with you on that. Something isn't right and even the Captain thinks so... But she has her orders and she passed them on to me. And now I'm telling you that you can't come."

"Well, if you won't take me, take Crewman Kaso. She's a hell of a fighter and has better instincts than anyone you have." Crewman Kaso took a more aggressive posture and hissed. "See, she's ready to go."

For a few seconds Ana thought Jax was kidding but then she realized that he wasn't. She chose her words carefully. "Jax, I'm sure she's capable but I don't think I could come back and face you if something happened to her."

She could see the unease in his face. "Look, when I get back I'll make you a nice dinner and we'll spend the evening in the holodeck with our Hollywood program and um, you know."

He smiled. "Yes, I know the 'um, you know' part of our evening quite well."

She walked up to him and wrapped her arms around his neck. "I'll be okay. I'm trained for this kind of work." He put his arms around her waist. She kissed him for a few seconds and moved her head back. "More of that when I get back."

"Is that a promise?"

"It sure is" she replied as she unwrapped her arms as started to look around the room. "I should be gone for no more than six days."

As Ana walked into the bedroom, Jax couldn't escape the thought that this was the last day he would see his wife alive."

Chapter 4

In the thirty-six hours since the security team left for Toriga IV, a dozen new science ships from various worlds had converged on Ostara System and more were on the way. It was becoming a nightmare for the three Federation ships to manage.

During Capt. Aziz' morning shift, Adm. Merino hailed the three science vessels. "Captains, the Talesian Brotherhood has launched an attack on Algerion Prime." All three captains had shocked looks on their faces. "The *Georgetown* has been ordered to that system to assist… I want Captains Stanton and Liebowitz to transfer their research crews to the *Fermi* immediately and then travel to Toriga IV at maximum warp. You should be there in less than eight hours."

"But Admiral, shouldn't I assist the other ships," asked Capt. Aziz sounding like someone who was being purposely ignored?

"You are assisting them by taking their scientists" replied the admiral brusquely. Catching herself, her voice eased. "Captain Aziz, there are over forty ships in the Ostara system and growing. Your ship will be the only one protecting those ships in the event something unexpected happens." Capt. Aziz didn't like the way that was worded.

The admiral continued: "The *Seleya* will rendezvous with you at eighteen hours. Until then, stay vigilant."

Capt. Aziz became even more troubled with the admiral's last statement.

The admiral then addressed all the captains. "I won't go into details now but will provide a briefing when you are on your way to Toriga IV. Merino out." The screen blackened.

Capt. Aziz informed her science teams that they would be receiving the science teams from the *Sagan* and the *Tyson*. As expected, there was grumbling from her scientists about others using their equipment and various other matters. Capt. Aziz calmly told them that if anyone failed to cooperate, they would be confined to quarters for the rest of the mission. The grumbling ended immediately.

Fifteen minutes later the science teams from the *Sagan* beamed aboard the *Fermi* followed closely by the *Tyson's* scientists. As soon as the *Fermi* had received the last scientist, both ships went into warp and vanished.

Chapter 5

Lt. Nandi was in Engineering later that day talking to his commanding officer, Lt. Cmdr. Adele Klein, when for no apparent reason he stopped talking in mid-sentence. His head snapped back and the blood began to rush from his face as his head slowly began to fall forward. From his lips Lt. Cmdr. Klein could barely hear him mutter the word “Ana” as his body began to slump forward.

Reflexively, she stretched out her arms and stopped his forward momentum when the palms of her hands pushed against his shoulders.

“Jax. Are you okay?”

Lt. Nandi quickly regained his senses when he felt the pressure on his shoulders and heard Lt. Cmdr. Klein’s voice.

“Uh, yes... I’m fine but Ana and her team” he said with the voice of someone who had just experienced a great loss.

“What about them?”

“I’m not exactly sure but something terrible has happened to them?”

“How do you know?” she asked.

“I don’t know how. I just know” he said excitedly. He had broken into a sweat.

Thinking fast she tapped on her communicator. “Lt. Cmdr. Klein to bridge.”

“Bridge here” came the voice of Capt. Aziz.

“Have you heard from the away team?”

There was a pause for a few seconds. “The last I heard from them was around three hours ago... Are you expecting to hear from them?”

“No... but could you let me know the next time they contact the ship?”

”Lt. Commander, is there anything wrong?”

“I’m not sure, Captain. It may be nothing.”

There was a long pause from the bridge. "We'll let you know when we hear from them."

"Thank you, Captain. Klein out."

Less than an hour after Lt. Cmdr. Klein hailed the bridge the *Fermi* received a transmission from Toriga IV that the Talesian Brotherhood had attacked one of the planet's secure facilities with a much larger than expected force. During the fighting that ensued on the planet's surface, several of the Starfleet Security personnel were killed along with many planetary defense force members. There was little information beyond that but they should have more by the time the *Sagan* and *Tyson* arrived at the planet.

Four hours later Capt. Aziz along with her command officers sat in her ready room watching Gen. Rusev, the commanding officer of planetary defenses on her viewscreen. The general was giving a briefing of the events that took place during the day. Captains Stanton and Liebowitz had arrived at the planet half an hour earlier and were now sitting in a conference room with Gen. Rusev along with their first officers. Adm. Merino could also be seen on the viewscreen sitting in her office.

"This has been a dark day for our planet," said Gen. Rusev with a demoralized look on his face. "We were helpless to defend ourselves without the assistance of a Federation starship." His face went from dejection to anger. "Why did your starship have to leave the area?"

Adm. Merino paused before she spoke. "General. As you know the intelligence we had on the Talesian Brotherhood was that they only had from 15 to 20 ships at their disposal. When they attacked Algerion Prime with fourteen ships, it was assumed that the intelligence on attacking Toriga IV was a ruse to draw the *Georgetown* away from their real target." She shook her head. "We seem to have grossly underestimated the size of the Brotherhood's fleet and their ability to attack much larger targets."

Capt. Standish interrupted. "Admiral, where is the *Georgetown* now?"

"The *Georgetown* is currently in pursuit of the Brotherhood ships that attacked Algerion Prime. They hope to intercept the ships before they reach the Typhon Expanse. If they don't we'll have to wait until they come out again... There are three more starships heading for the Expanse but it is unlikely that they will reach it in time to prevent the pirates from entering it."

Capt. Leibowitz interrupted. "Admiral, there is no known technology that can allow a starship to maneuver in a nebula but they seem to come and go as they please."

"Yes, that is true, Captain. It would be nice if we could capture one of their ships but the one time we were able to disable one, it self-destructed."

Adm. Merino turned her attention back to Gen Rusev. "General. I'm deeply saddened by the loss of life and property on your planet but I must remind you that there were a number of Starfleet Security personnel who lost their lives today defending your planet."

Capt. Aziz' eyes perked up when she heard the admiral mention Starfleet casualties. She wanted to know the status of her crewmen.

Gen. Rusev responded to the admiral. "Admiral, we mourn the deaths of your security team as we mourn our own. They acquitted themselves well and because of them we were able to take prisoners."

Capt. Aziz could not restrain herself from asking questions any longer. "Excuse me General but how many of our crewmen were killed today and what were their names?"

"The numbers we have are six confirmed dead, nine injured and eight missing presumed to be dead." Capt. Aziz's head dropped as she slumped in the chair. "The eight missing are the ones who entered the medical warehouse seconds before a rocket struck it." The general's head dropped. "The building was still burning when this briefing started."

There was silence for a good fifteen seconds before Adm. Merino asked: "When can you provide us with their names and status?"

"Admiral" replied Capt. Stanton. "Capt. Liebowitz and I have sent our second officers to the area. We should have the names shortly."

Capt. Aziz did the quick math. At best, all of her crewmen would have survived with three injured. At worst, none of her crewmen would have survived. Her instincts of not liking the idea of sending them angered her but she would not have become captain if she only obeyed orders she liked.

Adm. Merino ended the briefing by telling Capt. Stanton to hail her as soon as the casualties were confirmed. Capt. Aziz looked at Cmdrs. Montgomery and Gintok: "Not a word about this to anyone." She shook her head. "It looks like I'm going to be the bearer of bad news."

Ninety minutes later the briefing resumed. The news was not good. Of the ten *Fermi* crewmembers that went to Toriga IV, only two survived, both crewmen who had been ordered to guard prisoners while the others began a sweep of the medical warehouse. Capt. Aziz and her officers sat in their chairs in total shock when they heard the news. The captain took the news the worst because she had given the order for them to go on the mission.

This wasn't the first time she had had crewmen die under her command. During the Founder's War, she had assumed command of a joint Federation/Romulan force that was trapped on a Class-L moon. Over seventy percent of the Federation forces died during the ensuing battles. Almost two-thirds of the troops that she had trained perished.

This was entirely different. This time she had to stay behind and wait helplessly as members of her crew were put into a life and death struggle with a hostile force. She would have much rather been on Toriga IV leading than sitting at a briefing hoping the people you command are not among the casualties. To her, it was torture.

At the end of the briefing Adm. Merino ordered Captains Stanton and Liebowitz to debrief all crewmen deemed 'fit for duty' at their earliest convenience. Injured crewmen would be debriefed when their doctors' gave their consent.

Of the eight crewmen killed, only two had spouses or other family members on board the *Fermi*. Lt. Cmdr. Klein had told the captain that Lt. Nandi had had a premonition about his wife's death so she had relieved him from duty until the status of the crewmen at Toriga IV had been resolved. After verifying that the lieutenant was in his quarters Capt. Aziz contacted Dr. Sornax to meet her in her ready room and from there, they would go to see Lt. Nandi first.

Dr. Sornax was a Denobulan who was not only the ship's surgeon but also doubled as the ship counselor. Ships the size of the *Fermi* seldom had a counselor so having one especially under these circumstances was a plus.

The captain and doctor proceeded down three decks to Lt. Nandi's quarters and pressed the buzzer. A few seconds later, a voice from inside the apartment bade them enter. When the captain and doctor entered, Lt. Nandi was sitting on the far left side of his living room sofa scratching the head of his Bajoran cat, Crewman Kaso. They were listening to some beautiful but mournful music that Capt. Aziz had heard somewhere before.

The cat was the first to react with a hiss. Lt. Nandi looked over at the cat and said "At ease, Crewman" as he stood up quickly while saying, "Computer, freeze music." Then looking at the two officers, he said "Captain. Doctor... I was right, she is dead."

Capt. Aziz was caught off-guard by his frankness. "Yes, Lieutenant, it's true."

His eyes focused on the floor. "How many others?"

"Seven."

"Damn!" He paused "How did they die?"

"A rocket hit the building they were in. There was a fire that engulfed the building."

"So, does that mean my wife's body won't be coming back to the ship?"

Capt. Aziz hesitated. She hadn't thought about how she would answer that particular question. "I'm not sure... It was a huge blaze."

Lt. Nandi just stood there for a few seconds not saying anything. Then, snapping out of his trancelike state, he said "The only thing worse than being told this is having to tell her parents."

"Well, if you'd like both the doctor and I are available to be with you when you tell them."

He looked at the doctor and captain. "Thank you but it's probably best if I do it alone."

"I understand" replied the captain. "If there is anything the doctor or I can do for you just let us know."

He looked at the doctor. "You wouldn't happen to have a bottle of Romulan Ale, would you?" he asked with a smile.

The doctor shook his head. "Not even for medicinal purposes, I'm afraid."

"Too bad. A little Miles Davis and a lot of Romulan Ale would be great for what ails me right now." The doctor and captain had no idea who or what Miles Davis was.

"If I had any, I'd be willing to join you" replied the doctor.

"Well, if you get any. Let me know and we can talk and drink."

"I'll let you know."

Lt. Nandi turned toward the captain. "Sorry, Captain. I didn't mean to exclude you but I believe you don't imbibe."

"No, Lieutenant. I don't... But you're still welcome to talk at any time."

"First let me look at the mission logs and the debriefing reports and I may take you up on the invitation."

Capt. Aziz thought his response was a little strange but if it would help him through his loss, she would not interfere. "I look forward to us speaking, Lieutenant," said the captain with a smile.

The lieutenant smiled back. "I know you have others to talk to so I'll let you go."

The captain began to turn toward the door but halted. "Oh, I've informed Lieutenant Commander Klein to let you take off as much time as needed."

"Thanks, Captain but that's not necessary. I'd rather keep myself busy than sitting around doing nothing."

"Maybe so." She turned to look at the doctor. "Well, we better let the lieutenant get some rest."

"Computer, resume music," said Lt. Nandi. The mournful music began where it left off.

Capt. Aziz probably shouldn't but she had to ask "Lieutenant, what is that music?"

"Oh, it's the second movement of Beethoven's Eroica Symphony. It seemed appropriate a little while ago and it's even more so now."

The captain listened for a few more seconds. "It's very beautiful. I'll have to listen to it when I get the chance." She smiled at the lieutenant and both she and the doctor turned and left the apartment.

As they walked away from the apartment, the captain turned to the doctor: "Well, what do you think?"

"He should be okay. But have Lieutenant Commander Klein keep an eye on him."

After the door closed, Lt. Nandi went into the bedroom and retrieved a metal container with dimensions of 32"x16"x6" from the bottom of his closet and placed it on the bed. As he sat down next to it he placed his thumbs on the container's heat sensitive locks and said to the computer that was activated "Recognize Nandi, Jackson, codename Scorpion" The locks scanned his thumbprints and released. He opened the lid and looked inside. He pulled out a sheath with straps on it about nine inches long containing what may have been a knife. He placed the sheath on his inner right forearm and secured it with the straps. He stretched out his arm and grabbed the two-inch hilt with the index and middle fingers of his left hand and secured the hilt with the heel of his hand. As he pulled the hilt out, what looked like an icepick six inches long became visible. With the icepick secure in his hand he moved it in front of his body and made movements like he was punching a large object in front of him. Satisfied that he was comfortable with his movements he placed the icepick back into its sheath and removed it from his arm.

The second item he removed from the container was a ten-inch long, one-inch wide mechanical device with straps on it. He strapped the mechanical device to his left inner forearm. The device had two sections to it which would extend or contract the length of the device depending on the movements on his left arm. The outer end of the device had a clamp on it.

With the device contracted, he removed a double-barreled derringer from the container and attached it to the clamp. He then adjusted the device so that the derringer sprang comfortably into his hand. After he was satisfied that the mechanism worked her removed the device and placed it back into the container.

The third item was an old western-style holster holding a disruptor shaped like a revolver once used centuries ago in the American West on Earth. He pulled out the disruptor and removed the power pack which was shaped like a cylinder of an old pistol and looked at it. The power was drained. He would have to recharge it. He replaced the power pack, holstered the disruptor and placed the holster on the bed.

The final object he removed from the container was a handmade Japanese Katana Sword. In a ritual-like manor, he retrieved the sword from the container, placing both hands under the bottom on the scabbard and top of the hilt before slowly lifting it out. He slowly eyed the weapon starting at the bottom and worked his way up. A smile crossed his face as he did this. He then moved the weapon to his right side and slowly slid the blade out of the scabbard. The light in the room reflected off of it as if he were holding a mirror. He admired the beauty of the workmanship.

In an era of starships that could literally destroy a planet, one would think something this meticulously built would be in a museum but if you looked more closely at the blood-stained leather hilt and the scratches and nicks in the blade you could tell that this had seen its share of action and had seen it recently.

After admiring it for several minutes he slowly slid the blade back in the hilt and returned the sword back into the container.

There it would remain until needed. The other three objects would figure heavily in the plan he was devising in his head.

By this time Crewman Kaso had come into the bedroom and had made herself comfortable on the bed. Jax looked at the cat and smiled. "Well, Crewman, it looks like I have one more fight in me."

The cat purred in contentment

Chapter 6

The *USS Seleya* remained in the Ostara System until the *Sagan* and *Tyson* returned from Toriga IV three days after the attack. As soon as the two ships entered the system, the *Seleya* set a course to the area where they thought the Talesian Brotherhood launched their attack and would begin searching for clues.

When the Sagan got within transporter range it beamed the *Fermi*'s only 'fit for duty' survivor, Petty Officer Tavis Winters, back to his ship. The *Fermi*'s only other survivor, Crewman Lynch, had to remain of Toriga IV because of the extent of her injuries. Doctors on the planet were optimistic of her making a full recovery but for now, bed rest and rehab was what the crewman needed.

Four days after the attack on Toriga IV, a memorial service was held on the *Fermi* for the eight crewmen who were lost in the attack. It was a very solemn ceremony for the ship's crew but what struck everyone as strange was that only a handful of scientists actually knew any of the deceased crewmen. One would think that for being in an enclosed area for weeks at a time, one would get to know most of the people on board.

However, this was not the case. The scientists, in general, were so absorbed in their work that they tended to take the running of the ship for granted and considered the crew as inconsequential to their work. The only positive thing about this whole tragedy was that the majority of scientists decided to take the time and get to know their shipmates and not live in the bubble they were used to.

Ten days after the attack on Toriga IV, Cmdr. Montgomery informed Capt. Aziz that Lt. Nandi wished to speak with her. Capt. Aziz had wondered why she hadn't heard from him but given what he had told her when she had informed him of his wife's death, she assumed he had completed all the research he was going to do. She informed the commander to schedule a meeting at 0900 hours the following day.

The next day's meeting between captain and lieutenant was amazingly brief. All he requested was that she contact an Adm. Blaine for him and he would explain everything when the three officers met. Lt. Nandi's directness had once again thrown Capt. Aziz' off-guard and she sat there with her mouth open for a few seconds not knowing exactly what to say.

Capt. Aziz didn't know Adm. Blaine. In fact, she had never heard of Adm. Blaine before their meeting. Now she was being asked to contact a Starfleet Admiral she had never heard of for a reason she was not aware of.

Admirals were temperamental. They didn't like minions like her calling out of the blue just because one of her subordinates asked her to do it. She thought the least she could do was contact her CO, Adm. Merino, and have her contact the admiral.

"Lieutenant, you're asking an awful lot and not giving me a good reason to do it."

"I know, Captain but everything will be explained to you when we meet with Admiral Blaine."

"So who exactly is Adm. Blaine?"

"He's in Starfleet Security."

"And what exactly does he do?"

"I'm sorry, Captain but I can't answer that question."

Capt. Aziz was starting to become annoyed. "And why not?"

"Because it's classified."

This comment really irked her. "Classified! How can the position of a Starfleet Admiral be classified?"

"There are many Starfleet positions that are classified. You just don't know about them" he said with a calm voice.

"I'm beginning to think we shouldn't have had this conversation" she replied without thinking.

"I must admit that it is a request that most Starfleet Captains never hear but I want to assure you that the reason why I'm making this request will be explained when we meet with the admiral."

She sighed. “Okay. Let me think about it and I’ll get back to you... Dismissed.”

“Thank you, Captain.” He got up to leave and stopped. “Oh, Captain?”

“What” she replied in an irritated voice?

“I would suggest that you not make inquiries about Adm. Blaine.”

“And why not?”

“For now, the less known, the better.” He turned and left the room.

Headaches had been cured centuries ago but today, Capt. Aziz had the mother of all headaches. Her only wish was that this Adm. Blaine would not know who Lt. Nandi was and she would never have to deal with this again.

At 1300 hours the following afternoon, Lt. Cmdr. Klein informed Lt. Nandi that the captain had scheduled a meeting with him at 1700 hours. He thanked the Lt. Cmdr. and continued with his work assignment until his shift was over.

At 1700 hours Lt. Nandi entered Capt. Aziz’ ready room and sat down. Two minutes later the face of Adm. Harold Blaine appeared on the screen. Adm. Blaine looked to be around fifty years old with salt and pepper hair, brown eyes and was clean-shaven. He was seated but from what she could see he appeared to be in excellent physical condition. When he spoke, he had a deep baritone voice which in a way was almost hypnotic.

When he saw Lt. Nandi, he smiled widely and said: “Jax, it’s good to see you.” His smile faded and his voice took a more somber tone. “I’m sorry to hear about your wife. She was a good one... Much too good for you.”

“Thanks, Admiral” Lt. Nandi replied. “I can’t disagree with you on her being a good one.”

Capt. Aziz was beginning to wonder why she was even there when Adm. Blaine turned his attention to her. “Captain, you are dismissed,” he said calmly.

It was like being hit by a two-by-four. *Did he just tell me to get out of my own ready room*? She was about to say something she knew she was going to regret but she didn't care. But before she opened her mouth, Lt. Nandi cut in. "Admiral, no. We need her to stay."

The admiral paused. "Are you sure about that?"

"Indeed I am, Admiral."

"Very well." The admiral looked directly at Capt. Aziz. "Captain, I want you to understand that anything said from here on in is confidential. If you speak to anyone not in this room about what is being discussed, then your meteoric rise through the ranks will come to a screeching halt... Do I make myself clear?"

Capt. Aziz was already angry but she knew now that Adm. Blaine was dead serious when he issued that threat. Fortunately, the diplomat in her overruled the warrior in her and she replied: "Understood, Admiral."

"Good." He shifted his attention to Lt. Nandi. "Now, Jax, what's up?"

"I'm going after Kradik Krell."

Capt. Aziz' mouth dropped open. *He must have gotten ahold of that bottle of Romulan Ale he was asking for* was the first thing that came to mind. But then she realized that she too wanted to get Krell for killing some of her shipmates before she joined Starfleet. She had had countless nightmares about that day over the years and had vowed to bring Krell to justice. Now, sitting next to her was someone who was either extremely brave or incredibly suicidal. Her bet was on the latter.

Adm. Blaine remained calm. "I thought you had a job?"

"You can get someone else to do that" replied the lieutenant.

"True, but I would prefer you." He hesitated to process what he had heard. "Why are you telling me you want to commit suicide?"

"Because I need all the information you have on the Talesian Brotherhood."

The admiral chuckled. "You are serious."

"Yes, I am."

He mulled over the request. "I can't order you not to go because you'll do it anyhow." He hesitated. "Okay, I'll give you what we have but it isn't much."

"I figured that but what about the Romulans?"

Capt. Aziz' jaw almost hit the table. *The Romulans? Why would this admiral be talking to the Romulans? No one has heard from them in over a year.*

Adm. Blaine acted like the lieutenant's request was nothing out of the ordinary. "Why don't you ask for something more doable, like intergalactic peace and brotherhood?" He studied the lieutenant's expression which hadn't wavered. "I can ask but I not sure they would be willing to help."

"The Romulans haven't been immune to the Brotherhood's exploits," said the lieutenant. "I'm sure that they want them as bad as we do."

"That's probably true but I'm pretty sure that they would prefer doing it themselves."

"True but they haven't done it so far and neither have we." Lt. Nandi paused. "Now, if you tell them that I'm going in after them, they might be more receptive."

The admiral chuckled. "Now that will really pique their interest. They'll be really disappointed that they didn't kill you six years ago."

Wait a minute. The Romulans tried to kill Lieutenant Nandi thought Capt. Aziz excitedly.

"They've been disappointed before." Lt. Nandi hesitated. "If it weren't for this I would have preferred staying dead."

"I understand what you're saying," said the admiral. "But from a Tal Shiar perspective, this could work out. If you kill Krell, they're happy and if Krell kills you, they're happy and if both of you are dead, they'll declare a national holiday."

"It's a 'win-win' situation for them. How can they turn you down" replied the lieutenant?

Capt. Aziz sat there dumbfounded. She thought she knew how Starfleet worked but what she was hearing was beyond anything she could have imagined. It was frightening and intriguing at the same time. She tried to erase the 'intrigue' notion out of her head.

The frightening thing was that a Starfleet admiral was assisting another officer in going on a suicide mission. That part had happened countless times before, most likely on any planet that ever had a military but never would she have imagined that they would take such a cavalier attitude about someone being sent to his death.

"Okay, I'll ask them. Anything else" asked the admiral?

"Yes. I was thinking that if I go in alone, I'll kill Krell and probably some of his lieutenants before they get me. That may disrupt the Brotherhood but it won't destroy them... Now if you can get me a strike team to go in with me, we may have the opportunity to capture Krell and do enough damage to their organization that will force them out of the Expanse."

The Admiral dropped his head and shook it. "On paper that sounds like a good idea. But where are you going to find anyone crazy enough to volunteer for a mission that's doomed to failure?"

The lieutenant smiled. "I think I can find a few volunteers."

The admiral's body straightened and his head snapped back. "No. You're kidding. Not them. Some of them are older than you."

"True but they're probably as bored as me. It's not right for people like us to die in our sleep from old age."

"Okay, assuming you can get your volunteers, how are you going to get in and out of the Expanse?"

"Maybe our friends the Romulans can help us with that... at least as far as getting us in. They could chase our ship into the Expanse or something like that. It would have to look real or the Brotherhood might drop us off in the middle of the Expanse and let us fend for ourselves."

"I'll see if they'll cooperate." The admiral hesitated. "That takes care of getting in. Now, how do you get out? The Romulans again?"

"No way. If they saw a ship carrying the Poison Clan and Kradik Krell, they'd just destroy it and go about their business." Lt. Nandi looked over at Capt. Aziz. "That's where you come in, Captain."

This caught the captain off guard. She was still trying to figure out what a Poison Clan was. "Huh? Me?" she asked.

"Well, you and the *Fermi*."

"I don't understand."

"Someone has to cover our back once we're out of the Expanse. Who better than you?"

Capt. Aziz was speechless. She just sat there with her mouth open. This gave the admiral a chance to speak. "Jax, you know we have larger more destructive vessels at our disposal."

"I know but we don't want to get into a shooting war with the Romulans. If we send a Galaxy Class starship to intimidate a scout ship, the Romulans are going to take that personally. But if they see a science ship, they'll probably underestimate the capabilities of its captain and we can use that against them." He turned his head toward the captain and smiled.

She looked him in the face. "Lieutenant, I'm flattered by your confidence in me but the *Fermi* is not a warship."

"In your hands, she's a formidable opponent for any other ship."

Capt. Aziz didn't know how to respond.

"You seem to have everything well thought out, Jax," said the admiral. "Anything else?"

"Yes, a couple of things. First, a ship."

"I think we can come up with something."

"I don't want something. I need something special."

"What do you consider special?"

"We'll talk about it later."

"Okay. And your second thing?"

The lieutenant looked at the captain. "I need to talk with Petty Officer Winters." She looked puzzled. He continued. "He's lying about something... Well, maybe not lying but he's omitting something that could clarify a few things."

"I can have you meet with him at any time" she replied.

"Thanks, but I need you there too." He could see she didn't think it was necessary, He continued. "It will probably involve you at some point."

"I'll arrange it" she replied.

He turned toward the admiral. "I think that's about all for now. Thanks, Admiral."

"Nice to see you, Jax. I hope this isn't the last time I do." He turned his attention to Capt. Aziz. "Captain, there are a few things we need to discuss."

Lt. Nandi rose and left the room.

After he left Adm. Blaine said "It appears that you've become involved in something way beyond your security grade. I would expect that you treat what you've heard here confidentially?"

"I will Admiral but what I'm hearing sounds like you're about to break every Starfleet regulation."

The admiral smiled. "Well, every 'written' Starfleet regulation."

"I don't understand, Admiral."

"Captain, let's just say every government no matter how good or bad has a dark side or as we call it 'an Underbelly'. That Underbelly is there to protect the interest of the government when all other peaceful negotiations have failed."

"I don't think I like this, Sir."

"Most people don't." He paused. "You were a military history major if I'm not mistaken?"

"That's correct."

"So where would Earth be at this point in time if it didn't have organizations like the OSS, CIA, MI6, and others?"

She thought about it for a moment and replied: "Probably a lot worse off."

"Exactly... Just remember that I'm not asking you to do anything that betrays your Starfleet oath. I just need you to quietly assist Lt. Nandi so he can perform his mission."

She thought again about what the Talesian Brotherhood had done to her shipmates and said "Okay, Admiral. I'll give him whatever he needs." She hesitated as though she had completely forgotten something important. When the thought came to her she had an embarrassed look on her face. "Admiral, what am I supposed to tell Admiral Merino?"

"I will inform her at the appropriate time."

Capt. Aziz wasn't quite sure what would be considered an appropriate time but he had assumed the responsibility of telling her superior."

"Now do you have any more questions?"

She hesitated. "Admiral, I have two questions." She took a breath. "From what I'm heard these past few minutes you've planted Lt. Nandi on my ship. Why?"

"That is a Starfleet Security concern, not yours. Do I make myself clear, Captain?"

She wasn't expecting such a firm retort. "Extremely clear, Admiral."

"Good, now what is your second question?"

"What sort of man do I have on my ship?"

The admiral leaned forward in his chair. "He's not a man. He's a weapon."

That comment turned her cold. She began to realize that she was becoming involved with a side of Starfleet that she had once heard about when she was entering her second year at the Academy. At that time she thought that the stories about a secret organization within Starfleet were made up by upperclassmen to keep you focused on the Federation's core principles, just like parents on most planets warn their children about entities that will do them harm if they are bad. She was beginning not to like this.

Chapter 7

Two days later, Capt. Aziz, Lt. Nandi and Petty Officer Winters met in the captain's ready room. To avoid suspicion by the bridge officers, Capt. Aziz told them that Lt. Nandi would feel better if he had a first-hand account of what happened on Toriga IV. Her officers thought it a little unusual but understood that people deal with loss in different ways.

Petty Officer First Class Tavis Winters enlisted in Starfleet nine years ago when hostilities between the Federation and the Klingon Empire began. By the time he was out of basic training, the war with the Klingons had ended and the Dominion War had begun. During that war, he saw more than his share of action against the Cardassians and the Breen and received several commendations for bravery. He was on one of the many troop ships awaiting the ground assault on Cardassia Prime when the war ended. He was promoted to Petty Officer Second Class at the end of the war and Petty Officer First Class three years ago. He is 6'2" tall, 190 lbs. with short black curly hair and a medium brown complexion.

Capt. Aziz informed PO Winters that Lt. Nandi would be interviewing him about the events on Toriga IV. He found that strange but he didn't disapprove. She looked up: "Computer, please begin recording the interview with Petty Officer Tavis Winters." Then she sat back and paid close attention to the Petty Officer's body language.

The Petty Officer first gave his sympathies to Lt. Nandi and told him that he wished he could have done more.

"Thank you, Petty Officer but that's where I want to begin."

PO Winters was surprised at his frankness. "Okay, Lieutenant."

"I'm wondering why your team went into the building in the first place?"

"We were having a running firefight at the warehouse complex with a dozen or so pirates. We managed to kill two of them and stun and capture two others. The remaining pirates ran into one of the warehouses. That's when your wife, the lieutenant, decided to follow them in."

"Didn't you think that was odd?"

"I don't understand the question."

"Why would you go into a warehouse loaded with medical equipment and who knows what else when the people you were chasing could just beam out of the building once they went inside?"

"A little, I guess but in the heat of the moment the decision was made to continue the pursuit."

"Which you did." Lt. Nandi paused and went into another line of questioning. "Why didn't you go in?"

Capt. Aziz noticed that that question caused the PO's face to contort slightly. "The lieutenant ordered me and Crewman Lynch to stay with the prisoners."

"Why you?" The PO's face became flush. "Why would the person with the most combat experience be ordered to stay outside and guard prisoners when your most inexperienced crewmen could have done that?"

The PO began to sweat. "I'm not sure. She just gave the order."

"And you didn't voice an opinion one way or another."

"No, I didn't, Sir."

"So you think it was sound tactics?"

He hesitated. "No, Sir. I didn't."

"And you didn't say anything?"

His breathing became heavy. "Uh, no, Sir. I didn't."

"You're a liar" replied Lt. Nandi with a firm, cold voice.

"Lieutenant" snapped Capt. Aziz angrily.

Lt. Nandi turned toward her and raised his hand at the wrist. "Captain. This is my interview. Please let me complete it."

She was annoyed with his response but she knew that PO Winters was purposefully withholding the truth. She eased back in her chair and let him continue.

"Thank you, Captain." He turned his attention back to PO Winters whose face was flush and sweating profusely. "Now, where was I? Oh, yes, I had just called you a liar. What do you have to say about that?"

He was angry. He was scared. He wanted to be somewhere else. "Nothing, Sir."

Lt. Nandi moved his chair closer to him making the Petty Officer even more nervous. "I have this theory about what happened that day. Would you like to hear it?" PO Winters remained silent.

Lt. Nandi glanced over at Capt. Aziz who was leaning forward in her chair waiting to hear what came next. He then looked back at PO Winters. "I'll take your silence as meaning 'Yes'." PO Winters dropped his head.

"On that day everything happened as you said until you got to the warehouse." He paused to make the PO more uncomfortable. "When you got there your CO wanted to charge in but you thought it was a bad idea and told her so. For whatever reason, the conversation became heated and she ordered you to stay outside with Crewman Lynch to guard the prisoners. This probably didn't sit well with you but you followed your orders even though you knew you shouldn't. Minutes later the building exploded and your comrades were gone."

"You, Crewman Lynch and the prisoners were probably knocked to the ground by the explosion. You recovered quickly and noticed that Crewman Lynch had been hit by debris. The prisoners appeared to be stunned but alive."

"Is that what happened, Petty Officer?"

PO Winters had his hands cupping his face and was sobbing. With his voice shaking, he said "Yes, Sir. It is." He gathered himself. "I told her it was suicide to go in there but she wouldn't listen. I told her that if we were going in I should lead the team and she should stay outside." He had stopped sobbing and looked directly at Lt. Nandi. "She looked at me as if I were crazy. She said that a leader leads and if I didn't like it I should wait outside and guard the prisoners. It was torture to watch your friends go to their deaths for no reason."

Capt. Aziz had learned this lesson while she was a cadet at Starfleet Academy. She had been recommended for a leadership course where cadets were put in simulated combat scenarios.

One of the scenarios was ordering someone to stay behind and sacrifice their life so others could live. To her, it was the most difficult scenario in the course. You have a tendency to put yourself at risk first rather than someone else. One valuable thing she learned in doing this scenario was that you can't lead if you're dead.

"So, if that's what really happened, why did Crewman Lynch corroborate your story," asked Lt. Nandi?

"I was the first person she talked to when she became conscious. We agreed to the story in order to not make our CO look bad."

Capt. Aziz' eyebrows raised. She wouldn't have thought less of the lieutenant or petty officer if he had just told the truth. But then, it was a combat situation and people tend to react first and rationalize much later.

"I appreciate your wanting to protect my wife's decision but you shouldn't have diminished what you did on that day."

The PO looked puzzled, as did Capt. Aziz. "I don't understand" he replied.

"Well, you're in a combat situation and you're put in charge of guarding prisoners. You see the building your crewmen enter go up in flames and you see the crewman you're guarding prisoners with severely injured. It is not uncommon in situations like that for even the best-trained crewmen to lose focus and take the point of least resistance. But you didn't. You were able to deliver prisoners for questioning as well as make sure your crewmate received immediate medical attention." He paused. "I'm impressed."

Capt. Aziz took offense to Lt. Nandi implying that Starfleet personnel would mistreat prisoners but as a military history major and someone with the personal experience she knew that in combat situations there are only soldiers trying to survive and most would do anything to do that.

PO Winters eyes perked up on hearing this. "I uh, I didn't really give that any thought. We had orders to take prisoners, if possible."

"And you did, Petty Officer" interjected Capt. Aziz. "Well done."

The petty officer attempted to smile.

"Is there anything else, Lieutenant?" asked Capt. Aziz.

He turned toward the captain. "Just a couple more things, Captain. And I might add that they should be considered 'off the record'."

Capt. Aziz looked up. "Computer, stop recording this interview." The computer responded, "**Acknowledged**."

Lt. Nandi turned back to PO Winters. "So, how do you feel about the Talesian Brotherhood?"

Anger crossed the PO's face. "I owe them big time."

"Enough to put your life on the line?"

The PO thought the question strange but replied "I've put my life on the line for less. Why?"

Lt. Nandi leaned forward in his chair. "Petty Officer, what I'm going to tell you is confidential. If you repeat what I say to anyone outside of this room your career will be over and you'll spend the rest of your life in some godforsaken outpost doing menial chores. Do you understand?"

PO Winters sat there trying to process what he had just heard. It was like he had been spoken to in some alien language. Then he said, "Understood, Sir."

"Petty Officer, I'm leading a small team into the Typhon Expanse to either capture or kill Kradik Krell and destroy as much of the Talesian Brotherhood as possible."

The PO sat there for a minute with a blank stare on his face. Then a smile crossed his face and then he chuckled. "This is a joke, right?"

"This is not a joke."

"No offense, Sir but you're an engineer, not a combat soldier."

"I guess you could say that being an engineer is my alter ego."

The PO's smile faded. He looked directly into Lt. Nandi's eyes. "You're kidding?" The lieutenant said nothing. He turned toward Capt. Aziz. "He's kidding, right?"

"No, Petty Officer, he is not kidding."

He sat there with his hands between his open legs. After a minute of mulling it over, he said: "You know it's a suicide mission?"

"I wouldn't call it that but the probability of us coming back from it is not very good" replied the lieutenant.

"That bad, huh?"

"Yeah, that bad."

"What are our chances of getting Krell?"

"If we get close to him we'll get him... and that's a big 'If'."

He shook his head. "You sure don't make volunteering sound attractive."

"Would you prefer I lie to you?"

He thought over the question. "No, Sir. That would be worse."

Lt. Nandi straightened himself in his chair. "Look, Petty Officer, think about it. If you want to hear more, meet me in Holodeck 3 tonight at 2030 hours. If you're not interested, keep in mind that this conversation did not happen."

"Yes, Sir. I will." He looked at Capt. Aziz.

"Thank you for coming in Petty Officer. Your revised statement will be noted and added to your original debriefing statement." The PO's head dropped. "But keep in mind that you aren't the first person to protect a fallen comrade. Nor shall you be the last."

The PO rose to leave the room. "Oh, Petty Officer, one last thing," said the captain. He turned toward her. "We can't have our petty officers walking around with tears in their eyes, can we? It would be bad for morale."

PO Winters wiped the tears from his face and adjusted his tunic to look more presentable. When satisfied, he left the room.

"Why did you ask Petty Officer Winters to go on your mission," asked Capt. Aziz as she turned toward Lt. Nandi?

"For two reasons, I guess... First, he stays focused on the mission even when things aren't going well."

"That is true, Lieutenant. What's the second?"

"To get him off the ship."

Capt. Aziz looked surprised. "Why?"

"I know he's talked to counselors when he was on Toriga IV but I've seen that look in his eyes before. He needs redemption and he's not going to get it on this ship."

The captain couldn't disagree with the lieutenant's assessment.

Chapter 8

Six days after the meeting with Lt. Nandi and PO Winters, Capt. Aziz received special orders from Starfleet Security. PO Winters had been selected to take part in an eight-week advanced counter-terrorism program given at Starbase 152. He was to report for training in ten days.

These orders struck Capt. Aziz as being extremely peculiar. Capt. Aziz had not personally approved PO Winters attending any training classes nor had anyone in her command staff requested that he take this training, especially since most of the replacements for the crewmen killed on Toriga IV had not yet reported for duty. It was only two days ago that Lt. Lof Orora, the replacement for Lt. Shushunova-Nandi, had reported for duty on the *Fermi*. Losing an experienced petty officer for an extended period under these circumstances was something that she would have preferred not dealing with.

During that morning's scheduled staff meeting she asked if any of her command officers were aware of the orders for PO Winters. They were just as surprised as her. After the meeting, Capt. Aziz contacted Adm. sh'Rella office on Starbase 152 to get some clarification on the orders. She was directed to a Capt. Ranor who was less than forthcoming when it came to explaining how or why PO Winters was selected to participate in this training nor was he willing to explain exactly what the training entailed. The captain was only told that everything would be explained at a later date.

Capt. Aziz sat motionless in her chair for a few minutes after the viewscreen went blank trying to sort out the orders and the lack of transparency in having them explained. *Maybe it has something to do with Lt. Nandi's mission*, she thought. *That would explain the secrecy*. Her first thought was to just go ask him but once again she had to remind herself that even though she was the captain, she couldn't go up to just anyone on the ship and strike up a conversation. There were protocols to be maintained. She would have to wait until she heard from Lt. Nandi before she could come to any type of conclusion.

Her thoughts turned to her depleted security team and how PO Winter's absence would affect it. The only good thing about it was that they were still assigned to study the nova taking place in the Ostara system. Starfleet had assigned several larger starships to patrol the surrounding sectors of space near the Typhon Expanse to prevent any more incursions by the Talesian Brotherhood, so the probability of needing what security personnel she had was negligible.

The following day Capt. Aziz' suspicions were confirmed when Lt. Cmdr. Klein came to her with a request that Lt. Nandi be given a 60-day leave of absence. According to Lt. Cmdr. Klein, Lt. Nandi was finding it difficult to perform his duties since the death of his wife. He would spend his leave evaluating whether he wanted to continue as a member of Starfleet. As an aside, Lt. Cmdr. Klein told the captain that Lt. Nandi's performance far exceeded anyone in Engineering even though he considered himself distracted.

Capt. Aziz laughed to herself knowing that Lt. Nandi needed a good reason to leave the ship to go after the Brotherhood and this was as good as it gets. She approved the request and said he could leave as soon as his departure did not affect the functioning of the ship. Lt. Cmdr. Klein said that that would be in five to seven days. "Very good" replied the captain.

On the evening of the fifth day after Capt. Aziz approved Lt. Nandi's leave, the captain was on the floor in the living room of her quarters saying her nightly prayers. Reciting prayers five times-a-day like her religion prescribed was next to impossible for a person in her position, so having the opportunity to roll out your prayer rug and take as much time as needed to show your devotion was something she looked forward to at the end of the day.

She has almost finished when her doorbell rang. Frustrated by the interruption, she bade them entry. Lt. Nandi walked into the room first looking at an empty sofa. He then scanned the room and found her on the floor in a corner of the room. He was carrying the same container he stored his unique set of weapons in.

"Oh, sorry captain. I didn't mean to interrupt your stretching."

She shook her head and began to rise. "Actually, I was praying."

He looked puzzled. "Praying?"

She smiled. "Yes. You've heard of it, I assume?"

"Why, yes. I actually have but I'm seldom around anyone who actually does it."

Seeing that this conversation was going nowhere fast, she changed the subject. "What's in the container?"

He looked down at it. "I'll get to that later."

She was waiting for him to continue but he said nothing. "Can I help you with something?"

"Yes, Captain. First, let me apologize for coming to your quarters but I have a request that would be quite awkward if done in your ready room."

She didn't particularly like the sound of what he was saying. "Oh?"

"Uh, yes. I need something from you."

"Oh, what?"

"I need your mind," he said calmly.

"What!" She wasn't sure how to take what he said. Her instincts told her to take a defensive posture.

Seeing her body language made him laugh. "Oh, no, Captain. It's not what you think." He paused. "How do you think I'm going to let you know when to come for us?"

She had given it some thought off and on but she figured he would let her know eventually. "I assumed it would be a subspace message."

"Not quite." He hesitated to search for words. "I'm going to send you the message psychically."

"Psychically? There's nothing in your personnel file that says you're a psychic."

"There are a lot of omissions in my personnel file, Captain." She gave him a strange look that was hard to interpret but he knew it wasn't one of affection. He continued. "If I were to send an encoded subspace message to you, the Brotherhood may not know what it says but they will know I sent something. It would be easier for them just to kill me and my team rather than waste time trying to get information out of us. But if I send you a psychic message, no one will know but us."

What he said made sense but she still had a lot of questions. "We won't be in close proximity. How do you know psychic thoughts go that far?"

"There have been some interesting studies done in the past few years. Some scientists believe it's possible that psychic waves can travel great distances. Some don't... As always, more experimentation is needed."

She shook her head. "Well, that's not very reassuring."

"No, but that's all we got."

"So when should I expect to hear from you?"

"Probably five or six weeks. Seven tops."

"And after that?"

"You probably won't be hearing from me," he said glumly.

"You don't mince words, do you?"

"If we get Krell, it will be worth it" he replied trying to be upbeat.

She didn't feel the same. "One last question before I let you do this... Will we be able to communicate?"

"If you were a trained telepath, definitely. If you have some latent psychic abilities, maybe."

She hesitated and reluctantly said, "Okay, what do I have to do?"

"We should probably go over to the couch. You may feel a little woozy."

They walked over and sat on the couch facing each other. He put his hands on both sides of her face, his index fingers touching both her temples. He could feel her head jerk as he touched her. He assured her that she could relax. She was having a hard time believing him.

Truth be told she had difficulty being touched by members of the opposite sex. It was her religious upbringing. She was taught that men and women did not touch until marriage. That may be well and good in her little corner of Earth but once she left the rules changed. The pirates who tried to sell her into slavery didn't care. Her first coed self-defense class at Starfleet Academy didn't care. The Jem'Hadar who tried to kill her on Torsett II didn't care. In her mind, this was different.

As he probed her mind she could slowly hear his voice, first seeming to come out of his fingertips and then out of nowhere. She was surprised when she discovered that he had removed his hands from her head. She was even more surprised when the room started spinning. She laid her back against the sofa and took deep breaths.

He rose from the sofa and walked to the other side of the room. He then psychically said, *"Raise your right hand."* She heard him and obeyed. *"Now, raise your left hand."* She obeyed.

"Now, psychically, tell me how you feel?" He could see the strain on her face but she couldn't respond. He looked at her and smiled. "The important thing is that I can communicate with you."

In spite of her knowing she had no psychic powers, she was still disappointed when she couldn't communicate. Being as competitive as she was, she felt she was at a disadvantage.

She had regained her composure. "Lieutenant, before you leave can I ask you a question?" He nodded. "Can I assume that Petty Officer Winters is going with you?"

"He is." He smiled. "That evening after the debriefing, he came to the holodeck. He saw the training programs that I take and became convinced that I wasn't kidding."

"What about the training classes at Starbase 152?"

His smile faded. "The less you know the better."

She didn't like the answer but accepted it. "One last question. What if you don't make it?"

He took a deep breath. "Once our deaths have been confirmed, Starfleet Security will inform you that Petty Officer Wilson died in a training accident. I, on the other hand, will have decided to retire from Starfleet."

She looked blankly at him. “So, that’s how it works?”

“Pretty much... Even if we get Krell and his buddies in the process, we’ll never get credit for it.”

“Well, you should.”

“People who seek glory tend to die sooner in this profession. That’s why Klingons contract other species to do their spying.”

She had never thought of that but it did make sense.

He perked up. “Oh, I almost forgot. The container... I was wondering if you would hold on to it until I return.”

“Well, I guess I could do that but why me?”

“Because if I don’t return I’d like you to have what’s inside.”

She looked at him curiously wanting to ask what was in the container but she didn’t want to be too nosy.

He looked at her. “I see I’ve piqued your interest about the container... Don’t worry. It won’t explode or anything like that... You’re just the person who would best appreciate what’s in there and know what to do with it.”

She became more curious as he handed her the container. She looked it over and saw the locks. “How do I open it in case, uh?”

“I’ve imprinted it in your mind. If you believe I’m really dead, just hold the box and it will trigger the access codes.” He looked at the expression on her face that indicated that she was not happy with him for doing that. “Captain, I know you’re not thrilled with someone invading your thoughts but I would not have gotten you involved in any of this if the lives of so many beings in this part of space did not depend on my success.”

She knew he was right. It was hard to believe that so much depended on a handful of people doing something that worlds hadn’t accomplished.

Reluctantly, she said, “I guess you’re right.”

He smiled. “Well, Captain, I hope to see you in the not too distant future.”

“Yes, Lieutenant, I’ll be there when you need me.”

He smiled, turned and left her quarters.

Chapter 9

Four days later PO Winters arrived at Starbase 152 but instead of being beamed down to the planet, he was immediately beamed onto a nondescript vessel called the *Vagabond*. The *Vagabond* was a small freighter registered to a Boslic merchant. At least, that is what people were led to believe. In actuality, the *Vagabond* was a sophisticated high-tech vessel used by Section 31 mostly for spying but on occasions, it would transport items of questionable importance. This time it was carrying three passengers to a planet where Starfleet personnel were not particularly welcomed.

The first person he saw on the *Vagabond* was Lt. Nandi who was out of uniform. Sitting beside him was his Bajoran cat Crewman Kaso. The lieutenant smiled broadly at the petty officer as he stepped off the transporter pad. "Greetings Petty Officer. I take it your trip here was uneventful?"

"Yes, Sir. It was." He looked around the transporter room which doubled as a storage area. "This isn't exactly Starfleet issue."

"No. Not really... The Starfleet you know ended when you stepped on the transporter pad to come to the *Vagabond*. From now on this is the unofficial Starfleet, a part that very few regular Starfleet people get to see."

PO Winters swallowed hard. "I've heard talk about this but I never thought I'd be involved in it."

"You aren't yet" replied Lt. Nandi. "Before I tell you more, I need to ask you something."

"Fire away."

"Okay. As I said before the real Starfleet is down on the planet where there is an actual eight-week terrorist training course that begins tomorrow. You can either beam down and take the course or you can stay on this ship and put your life on the line without any chance of ever being recognized or rewarded for your efforts."

PO Winters head snapped to attention as he swallowed harder this time. "You come right to the point, don't you Lieutenant?"

"I don't want you having second thoughts about this once we get underway."

The petty officer stood there and thought about it for a good minute. Then he said "I've been having my share of nightmares since the firefight. I owe it to my crewmates and myself to make their deaths meaningful."

"Good," said Lt. Nandi. "Now there are a few things we need to clear up before we leave... First, from now on you will either call me Captain or Jax. If you make the mistake of calling me Lieutenant, it may put the team and the mission in jeopardy. Do you understand petty officer?"

"Understood, Lieu... uh, Captain." His face showed embarrassment.

Lt. Nandi shook his head, "I know. It's a trick question but there is no shortage of people out there who will sweet-talk you into giving them your mother's dowry." He paused. "Second, you're the low man on my team's totem pole and the other members of my team will give you orders. Obey them as you would me."

"Third and most important. When I give you an order, obey it. If I tell you to kill a woman holding a baby, kill her."

Winters looked shocked at his pronouncement.

"Winters, there are species that you've never encountered. Just because they look harmless doesn't mean that they are."

Winters thought about it for a few seconds and understood his reasoning. "Understood."

"Finally, we may be put in a situation where we might have to kill innocent civilians. Do it. If you don't the Brotherhood will kill you as well as the civilians."

This shook up Winters. Jax looked at him and said with a calm voice. "I know what you're thinking and you're right. But remember, if doing that gets us closer to Krell, we can avenge those deaths and a few thousand others."

Winters looked Jax in the eye. "How do you sleep?"

"A lot of times I don't." Jax sensed his uneasiness. "Having second thoughts?"

"Yes, but I have trouble sleeping already." He tried to smile.

"Good." Jax walked over to an instrument panel and pressed a communicator button. "Captain, let's get underway." The captain acknowledged him.

As he turned towards Winters he noticed him reflexively jump to his right side and look down. Crewman Kaso had begun to rub her body against Winters' left leg.

"Stand down, Crewman" Jax snapped. She hissed and began to move away. Embarrassingly, Jax said "Sorry. She's in heat and has caught your scent."

Winters regained his composure. "No problem. I just wasn't expecting that." He hesitated. "I was wondering. Why do you call her Crewman Kaso?"

"Because that's the name and rank she had when I first met her." Winters looked totally confused by the comment. Jax smiled. "It's a long story and a long trip. Maybe I'll fill you in on the details."

"Yeah. Okay." He decides to change the subject. "So where to and why?"

"Vexia III, to meet the rest of my team."

Chapter 10

Vexia III is a Class-M planet located in the Sierra Sector of the Alpha Quadrant. Even though the planet was well within Federation space, it was not part of the Federation and had no intentions of ever joining. The government was run by businessmen whose primary interest was to generate as much revenue for their planet and themselves as they could. As a result, Ferengi made up about twenty percent of the planet's population all eager to make their fortune. The only thing the government asked is that they receive 20% of the profits to keep the government operating.

You may imagine how difficult it must be for the government to collect their fair share of taxes from the Ferengi whose core beliefs are to lie, cheat and steal in order to earn a profit. In the beginning, this was a problem but over the years the government adapted to this problem and now Vexia III was proud to say that it had more auditors per capita than any other planet in the Alpha and Beta Quadrants. Tax cheats were dealt with severely. Lesser crimes like arms trafficking, fraud or money laundering had a habit of being overlooked as long as the state got its cut. Life was good. Profits were better.

The *Vagabond* orbited over Vexia's main city of Hraine long enough to beam down its two human passengers before it moved into a higher orbit around the planet. There it would stay in orbit until the team had assembled and were ready for the next phase of their mission.

Jax and Winters exited the central transporter building and spent the next ten minutes bargaining over the cost of a cab ride to their rendezvous point with a Ferengi cabbie. Jax turned down his offer to meet "Dabo girls so nice that you'd want to take one home to meet your parents" for only 20 strips of gold-pressed latinum more and settled on just being taken to the address discussed. "Too bad, human. You aren't going to get a better deal" said the cabbie as the vehicle began to move.

Winters had grown up on Mars and had spent his entire life before joining Starfleet inside the Federation. He had never seen anything remotely familiar to what he was looking at along the streets of Hraine. Bright lights, loud music, scantily-clad females or what Winters' thought might be females were everywhere. When he was in the Bajoran sector he thought the nightlife there was uninhibited. Hraine made that look like a prayer meeting. As they drove down the main street they passed by one particular establishment where the music was so loud his teeth began to vibrate. *If I survive this mission, I'm definitely coming back here,* he thought with a smile on his face.

The cab turned off the main strip and proceeded down a less busy side street stopping at the end of the block at a more subdued establishment called *The Beetle Snuff Saloon*. Both humans got out of the cab and were told that the agreed-upon fare was now 50% higher. Winters was surprised and impressed when Jax pulled the cabbie through his open window and placed his forearm firmly under the cabbie's chin. The cabbie suddenly recalled that he was in error and that the price agreed upon was indeed lower. Jax relieved the pressure and placed the money in the cabbie's jacket pocket, turned and headed for the saloon's entrance. Winters followed.

There is some unwritten law in the Universe that says that all establishments that predominantly sell alcoholic beverages look and smell the same inside. *The Beetle Snuff Saloon* was no exception to that law. Unlike the bars of the main strip, this was relatively small with a bar area of about 60'x40'. As you walked through the front entrance a 40-foot-long bar was to your left. There were sixteen bar stools in front of it, half currently being occupied. Before you got to the bar was a double swinging door which leads to the kitchen. Past the bar at the far end corner of the room was a table with six chairs. There were nine other such table combinations evenly spaced around the outside of the room, none being less than six feet away from its adjacent tables when the chairs were pulled out. These tables were not for drinking. They were for discussing business and discussing it with some degree of privacy. There were four tables already occupied with different species from different worlds talking about things that would probably cause your death if you accidentally overheard what they were saying.

You had to walk down two stairs to get the inner tables which were closer together and with varying numbers of chairs. In order to maintain the privacy of the customers in the 'private' area, a wood-like railing surrounded the inner tables except in front of the bar and at the far end of the lower area.

To their right was a stairway that went up. To where and for what purpose was unknown to Jax. Rumors had it that there was some high-stakes gambling that took place up there for clients who preferred to stay anonymous. No one really knew.

As the two humans walked into the saloon, Winters shivered and looked down at his hands. The hair on the back of his hands was standing up. "What's going on in here," he asked Jax?

Jax looked over at him. "Oh, that's part of their security system."

He looked at Jax as if he were joking. Jax smiled. "Look around the room and see if you can hear anyone's conversion?" Winters did as he was asked. Nothing. He could hear a loud group of men talking loudly at an inner-room table but he could not make out a word they said.

"Interesting" replied Winters.

"Yeah, and it prevents telepaths from reading your thoughts or someone making recordings of your conversations. There's also some technology that skewers any videos that you make."

"I see why you come here."

"Well, that and the fact you can get one of the best Margaritas made this side of Earth."

"Well, well. We don't get many humans in this place" said a voice to Jax' left.

He turned toward the voice and smiled: "They told me there was the most beautiful Ferengi female I would ever see here and I see they were right."

She smiled. "If I weren't married to that worthless loser over there, I'd take you to the back room for oo mox." Her head shifted in the direction of an older obese Ferengi male sitting at the bar sniffing beetle snuff.

"I have offered to put him out of his misery for you but you keep refusing."

"True but our son needs to have an example of what not to grow up and be." Both she and Jax laughed.

Jax turned toward Winters. "Oh, forgive me. Winters this is Drid. Drid, Winters." Both parties smiled and nodded.

"Drid is the proprietor of this establishment and I believe the first female Ferengi to open any type of business on this planet."

"Well, it took a lot of work and even more latinum but I have a place to call my own."

"You should be very proud of yourself" replied Winters. "So, tell me, how do you compete with the larger bars on the main strip?"

"I sell what they can't. Discretion... Oh, the other bars have back rooms and high security but you can come in here and say whatever you want to whomever you want as loudly as you want and someone six feet away can't hear you... You'd be surprised how many government officials show up here."

"Looks like you've got things figured out."

"So far. So good" she replied. She turned to Jax. "Take the table at the far right corner.' She pointed in that direction. "Oh, I take it you want your usual?"

"Is the Pope Catholic? You bet I do."

"What will you have?" looking at Winters.

"Do you have Earth beer?"

"There's a microbrewery on the planet that makes five different varieties of Earth beer?"

Winters had a smile on his face a mile wide. "If you have a dark ale, I'll volunteer to get rid of your husband for you."

Drid smiled "Make that 'yes' for the first and 'no' for the second." She turned and walked toward the bar.

As Jax and Winters walked past the three occupied tables in route to theirs, Winters tried to hear the conversations going on. Nothing. Sound but no substance.

Jax and Winters sat down at the table and waited for their drinks. They chit-chatted about nothing special or important. Winters was commenting on how deceptively comfortable the chairs were at the table. "It seems to adjust to whatever position I place my body."

"You have to remember that not everyone in the Universe is shaped like a human."

Winters pondered the obvious and was about to make a comment when he noticed the noise level in the bar had dropped to near silence. He looked at Jax, who seemed unalarmed, and then scanned the rest of the room. As his eyes reached the front entrance his head stopped and his mouth dropped.

There were two tall, slender but well-built humanoid-like males blocking the front entrance scanning the room as if they were looking for someone. The first was a Nausicaan.

Nausicaans were best known to be surly and ill-tempered who made excellent bodyguards for people who could afford them. They were also known to dabble in illicit trades such and piracy, arms smuggling, and murder. Nausicaans were not uncommon on Vexia III. It was said that you could tell the wealth of a businessman by the number of Nausicaan bodyguards he had.

In spite of them not being rare, it was strange that one would come into a bar like *The Beetle Snuff Saloon* accompanied by the second person. It was a Jem'Hadar soldier.

It was thought that all the Jem'Hadar had left the Alpha Quadrant through the Bajoran wormhole six years ago when the Dominion War ended. Besides being rare, no one quite knew how long the lifespan of a Jem'Hadar actually was. Winters sat there both fascinated and worried that either one of the two patrons would lose their temper or all hell would break loose.

The two newcomers took two steps forward and were about to step down into the inner section when the Nausicaan looked over at the bar and nodded at the bartender. The bartender nodded back and began concocting some beverage. As the two walked slowly through the inner tables, each table would stop talking and try not to stare. If someone did stare, the two would stop and stare back just long enough to make them nervous.

Winter tried not to stare so he began to look around the room. What he found extremely strange was that the patrons in the lower tables were transfixed with the two while the patrons in the upper tables carried on with their conversations as if nothing out of the ordinary was taking place.

At the far end of the room were stairs that led to the upper section which the two newcomers decided to take. When they reached the top they first looked to the left and found nothing of interest. They then turned right and saw Winters and Jax waiting patiently for their drinks. Well, at least Jax was. Winters was breaking into a sweat by now.

The two slowly walk up to Jax' table came to a halt and stared at them. Jax ignored them.

The Nausicaan laughed. "Look at the humans. They're usually all pink and fragile but these two seem to be a bit healthier with more color in their skin than the others."

"I've never liked humans. The last time I encountered them, they were running in the other direction" said the Jem'Hadar.

The Nausicaan laughed. "I heard that they're not very good to eat. What good are they?"

Jax slowly raised his head. "You know, my sister just lost her husband a few months ago and she's looking for a new one. When I saw a handsome devil like you come in I knew she'd be interested... Now you've gone and insulted all mankind, so I'm not going to give you her address."

Winters almost panicked. Jax stayed calm.

The Nausicaan didn't quite know if he had been insulted. He turned toward the Jem'Hadar. "I think we should teach these two a lesson."

Jax stood slowly, exaggerating his movements. He spread his arms out. "If you want some. Come get some."

The bar became silent again. Everyone was looking at the table in the far right corner waiting for something to happen. Even the other upper tables stopped their conversations to look. They couldn't hear what was going on but they knew it was going to be bad.

The Nausicaan turned toward Jax, took a step forward and spread his arms similar the Jax. Winters began to situate himself in his chair in order to get out quickly to fight.

Suddenly Jax and the Nausicaan smiled at each other and hugged. The Nausicaan lifted Jax off the ground and said "My friend. It has been a long time."

"Too long, buddy... Now, will you put me down before you break my back?" Jax' feet touched the ground seconds later.

Winters was halfway out of his chair not knowing whether to stand or sit. His mouth was open.

Jax turned toward the Jem'Hadar and smiled. They hugged like long lost friends.

"Well, old timer. You look pretty good for your age" said Jax jokingly.

"Thanks, my friend. I don't think any Jem'Hadar has ever reached nine years before."

"I can truthfully say that you don't look a day over seven."

"Thank you. I think."

Jax looked over at Winters who had figured out by then that there was not going to be any violence. "Relax, Winters. These are my friends." Pointing to the Jem'Hadar "This is Zitag'dur. And this good looking fellow here is Neer" pointing to the Nausicaan. "And this is Winters."

Both Neer and Zitag'dur looked him over closely. "He's kind of young to be going on a mission like this," said Neer.

"More appropriately, we're kind of old to be doing this" replied Jax.

"True," said Zitag'dur. "But if we die during this mission our lives will be worth it."

"I would prefer that we survive this one just like the others" replied Jax. He looked over at Winters. "You don't seem to be saying much?"

Winters looked at him. "I'm still trying to get a handle on all of this. I would have never guessed that a Nausicaan and a Jem'Hadar were working for the Federation."

"There's a lot of things that you wouldn't expect to be happening in Starfleet. When it comes to feigning ignorance about those things, Starfleet is in a class by itself."

As the four comrades seated themselves, Drid walked up carrying a tray with four drinks and a vial of with a white substance on it. She gave Jax his margarita, Winters his beer, Neer a large mug with some unknown concoction in it and Zitag'dur the vial. "It's something that the bartender cooked up. It will put hair on your chest" joked Drid. She then placed the last drink on the table in front of an empty chair as if there was still one more person to arrive. "Will there be anything else?"

Jax smiled. His drink was as large as a fishbowl. "I think this will keep us going for a little while."

She turned as if to walk away but only walked to the next table and placed the tray on it. Then she walked back to Jax' table and sat down.

Jax smiled and looked around the table. "You don't know how happy I am to see you all again." He then turned toward Winters. "Winters. You have just become part of the most successful strike teams the Federation has ever assembled. Welcome to the Poison Clan."

The comrades lifted their glasses and toasted each other.

"The Poison Clan rocks the world," they said in unison.

Chapter 11

The Maxima Shipyards is a Federation Facility orbiting Vanov II, a large Class L planet, in the Sierra Sector. Its main purpose is to strip decommissioned Starfleet vessels of their weapons, scientific equipment, electronics and precious metals for reuse. Sometimes the ships are completely disassembled but more often than not, the shells of the ships remain intact.

In addition to that, the shipyards stores ships that have been confiscated by Starfleet usually for being involved in criminal activity of some sort or have been stolen and are waiting to be reclaimed by the owner.

The *Vagabond* orbited Vanov II on the far side of the planet, away from the shipyards. Because of its sophisticated hull plating, it was nearly impossible to identify it unless you knew exactly what you were looking for. Over the next eight hours, the *Vagabond* would slowly move closer to the edge of the shipyards so it could beam its five passengers on board one of the confiscated vessels.

On board, the *Vagabond* Jax was giving a last-minute briefing to his team. “As you are aware, Starfleet has been cracking down on anyone suspected of being associated with the Talesian Brotherhood. They’re even investigating cases of criminals who are believed to be dead... Can you imagine that?” He chuckled. “One name that will conveniently be at the top of the list will be someone called Scorpion, who was the leader of a gang called the Poison Clan” The group roared their approval.

“In a little over an hour Starfleet will issue an alert through normal subspace informing Starfleet vessels that an attempt to capture the Poison Clan failed and they are at large. Starfleet believes that the Clan hijacked a Napean vessel in order to escape.”

“Twelve hours after that, Starfleet will issue another alert saying that a ship that may contain the Poison Clan has been stolen from the Maxima Shipyards. They will know this because they will find the warp signature of the same stolen Napean ship along the shipyard's perimeter."

"Do you mean that the *Vagabond* can imitate different warp signatures?" asked Winters.

"Winters, the *Vagabond* is one of the most technologically advanced ships in the Federation. It does everything but cloak itself." He chuckled. "Actually, it can hide its warp signature, so technically, sensors won't be able to see it."

"We wouldn't want the Romulans to think we're breaking any treaties, would we" joked Drid?

"Oh, no. Not us. We're the good guys and would never do anything like that" replied Jax. Everyone but Winters laughed.

Jax continued. "So we have about twelve hours to prep the ship and sneak through as much Federation space as we can before the alert is given."

Drid asked, "Doesn't it take eighteen hours to get to the Typhon Expanse?"

"It's going to take longer than that because we have to set a fake trail first." Winters looked confused. "There are some goodies on the ship that will help us do that" explained Jax.

Winters tried to process what he had heard. "Assuming that these 'goodies' work and we make it through Federation space to the Typhon Expanse, what then?"

"I was coming to that. As we get within range of the Expanse, a Starfleet Security ship will just happen to be in the vicinity of where we are. They will pursue but will be unable to catch us."

"Isn't that a bit convenient?"

"It definitely is. That's where the Romulans come in."

"Romulans!" asked Winters?

"Yep. Romulans." Jax took a breath. "See, the Brotherhood would probably be suspicious if only the Federation tried to stop us. But if the Romulans come after us, they're going to scratch their heads and wonder what's going on."

"Captain, how do we know the Romulans won't just destroy our ship? We haven't made too many friends in our dealings with the Empire" asked Drid.

"At the moment, they hate the Brotherhood far more than they do us. My only concern with them is what they'll do if or when we come out of the Expanse?"

"My guess is that they'll try to capture us. A public execution always keeps the populace happy" added Neer.

"True but that's where the *Fermi* comes in."

"I've heard of Captain Aziz' exploits but how good is she commanding a starship," asked Zitag'dur?

"I'm betting all of our lives that she's better in a captain's chair than she is on foot." The group sat there and reflected on what Jax said.

Jax continued. "Once we get in, we're supposed to hook up with a Romulan asset who will provide us with intelligence."

"Wait a minute," said Drid. "What Romulan asset? You know we work alone."

Jax shook his head. "We had no choice but to include a Romulan. They said they wouldn't cooperate unless we did." He paused. "My guess is they'll want to take credit for the operation if we're successful. Either that or the asset will try to kill us and take Krell for the Empire." He chuckled. "On the other hand, the Brotherhood may have already killed him and our only hope is that he had the courtesy not to spill the beans before he died."

"Romulans are very good at not divulging information under torture," said Zitag'dur with a satisfied look on his face. The others looked at him strangely as he reminisced about his wartime activities.

"Yeah, okay. On that cheery note. Any more questions?"

"Just one, Captain," said Winters. "We're assuming that the Brotherhood will know about us before we even arrive at the Expanse. How can you be so sure?"

"Because the Brotherhood has been using the Expanse as a refuge for the last twelve years. They come and go as they please and know where Federation and Romulan ships are before they expose themselves. They're pretty sophisticated. They'll know... The big question is will they fall for it?"

Jax looked around the room. "Be back here in 45 minutes. We've got a ship to steal."

The security system around the Maxima Shipyards was designed to detect a ship entering or leaving its perimeter. Once detected, ships and drones would be dispatched to investigate. Because of this, it was decided that they would beam the Clan into their new ship from a distance too far for a normal transporter.

In spite of the distance, the ship-to-ship transfer was uneventful. The team materialized on the deck of a small but impressive looking ship, at least from the inside, located in a cluster of ships around the same size.

"Ladies. Gentlemen. Welcome to the *Hellfire*" said Jax with a flourish. The movement of his wrist appeared to cause him pain.

"Captain, are you all right" asked Drid.

"I will be when I find a med-kit." He looked around for a first-aid kit and mumbled: "I knew she'd be angry when she found out I wasn't taking her on this mission."

"What did you expect from a Bajoran female?" asked Drid. "What's that ancient Earth saying 'Hell hath no fury as a woman scorned.'?"

"Yeah but most Bajoran females don't have two-inch fangs."

Jax found the first aid kit and injected an anesthetic into his arm with a hypo-spray. A few seconds later, he moved his wrist around with less discomfort.

The emergency lights were on but the bridge consoles and equipment were inactive. "How do we get this thing up and running" asked Drid.

"Easy" replied Jax. "Oh, Lucy. I'm home" he said in a half-singing manor.

The console lights began to flicker and the bridge lights illuminated. There was a slight whine from the ship's computers booting.

"**Please identify yourself,**" asked the computer in a female voice?

"Lucy, recognize Nandi, J. M. Captain. Beta Delta 35962 Epsilon."

"**Nandi, Captain, recognized. All bridge functions are under your command**."

"Lucy, recognize Drid, Commander, Omega Mu 92569 Zeta"

"**Drid, Commander, recognized**."

"Lucy, recognize Neer, Commander, Lambda Theta 42934 Tau"

"**Neer, Commander, recognized**."

"Lucy, recognize Zitag'dur, Lieutenant Commander, Beta Pi 22673 Xi"

"**Zitag'dur, Lieutenant Commander, recognized**."

There was a long pause before everyone looked at Winters. "Oh," he said a bit off guard. "Lucy, recognize Winters, T. R. Petty Officer, Kappa Psi 83546 Zeta"

"**Winters, Petty Officer, recognized**."

As they were recognized by Lucy, each crewman went to his station, Drid to Engineering; Neer to the helm and Zitag'dur to tactical.

Winters looked at Jax with a surprised look. "Captain. You mean, they're all Starfleet Officers?"

"Not all Starfleet Officers wear shiny uniforms and have a shower at the end of the day" replied Jax.

Winters shook his head and grinned. "This is going to take some getting used to."

"You can start by forgetting everything you just heard. Remember what I said about making one slip of the tongue."

"I did, Captain."

"Good."

Lucy, the computer interrupted "**Captain, all systems are fully operational and within normal parameters**."

"Good. How soon will we be ready to leave?"

"**Six point five zero minutes... Oh, it is good to be working with you again, Captain**."

"Thanks, Lucy. I've missed you too."

Winters looked at Jax. "Captain, that computer isn't artificial intelligence, is it?"

"That it is, my boy."

"But Starfleet doesn't..."

Jax interrupted. "Don't say it. We're breaking another Starfleet regulation..."

Winters saw the irritation in Jax' face and decided it was best to remain silent.

Jax sat down in the captain's chair and turned toward Zitag'dur who was sitting at a computer console against the starboard wall. "How soon do you think you can interface with the shipyard's main computer?"

"If we didn't already have the appropriate passwords, I'd say one hour, maybe more. But seeing that we do less than ten minutes."

"Good." Jax lifted his head. "Engine Room, status?"

"The engine is purring like Crewman Kaso after a good meal" replied Drid. "And you should see how they've run the phaser banks power through the engine. It looks like it could do some heavy damage to a Warbird."

"That's nice to know but I'd prefer not to find out... Anything, weapon wise, I should know about?"

"There are four photon torpedoes on board. Two fully weaponized and two loaded with the chemicals you asked for."

"Great. Do you need any help loading one of the chemical ones into the aft torpedo bay?"

"No, Captain. Everything is automated."

He looked forward toward Neer at the helm. "Neer, status?"

"The star charts are up to date. We can leave whenever you want."

Finally, Jax looked at Winters who was still standing. "Well, find yourself a seat and enjoy the ride."

Jax was waiting for Zitag'dur to give him the green light when a thought popped in his head. He sprang to his feet unexpectedly, catching everyone by surprise, and headed directly toward the cargo bay. As he scanned the bay his eyes finally locked on to the objects he had requested. On a rack were eight environmental suits of varying sizes. None of the suits fit any of the crew exactly because if the ship were stolen, why would they. Jax had Section 31 put eight suits in the *Hellfire* in case the Romulan agent was going to escape with them. Jax took a quick look at the suits' oxygen gauges to make sure they were all filled to capacity.

Just to the left of the suit rack was a stasis chamber about three feet by three feet by seven feet. Stasis chambers were not standard equipment on small vessels but this was the science vessel that supposedly would do deep space missions. If someone became ill and needed medical attention, they could be placed in the stasis chamber and put in suspended animation until the ship could reach a medical facility.

Boy, I hope we don't have to put Neer in this thing. It would be a really tight fit thought Jax as he opened the chamber and looked inside.

When Jax returned to the bridge Zitag'dur turned to him: "I'm in and awaiting orders."

"Neer, thrusters only. Point us toward the closest perimeter point and fire a quick burst so we coast out of the shipyard."

The *Hellfire* glided toward the perimeter. "Okay Zitag'dur, work your magic," said Jax. Zitag'dur began working on the computer console. "Captain, there will be disruption on the far side of the shipyards in eight seconds. Two seconds later we will breach the perimeter without them knowing it."

"Five, four, three, two, one," said Zitag'dur. On 'three' his computer console registered a disturbance at the most distant side of the shipyard. Two seconds later Zitag'dur said: "We have successfully cleared the perimeter and the computer glitch has been corrected."

"Now let's hope we don't accidentally run into any Starfleet vessels."

"So, what if we do" asked Winters?

"We either outrun them or fight them" replied Jax blankly.

Winters' head dropped. "Just like that?"

"Pretty much. They won't know that we're the good guys and we can't tell them."

"Oh." Winters sat there with his head down staring at the floor.

On board the *Fermi*, the bridge had just received an alert from Starfleet informing them Starfleet Security had raided the suspected hideout of a high-value group of criminals known as the

Poison Clan but were unable to capture them. The group, who was reported killed six years ago, is wanted by Starfleet for crimes that include kidnapping, robbery, and handling of stolen goods.

When Capt. Aziz heard the name of the criminals, her eyes lit up, so much so that her second officer, Cmdr. Gintok took notice.

"Captain, are you familiar with these bandits?"

She had to think quickly. "No, not personally but I recall hearing stories about them before I joined Starfleet." This response seemed sufficient enough to satisfy Cmdr. Gintok.

So, I guess Lieutenant Nandi and Petty Officer Winters are on their way to the Typhon Expanse thought the captain. *I hope they'll be successful.*

Twelve hours later the bridge received another alert informing them that the Poison Clan was believed to have stolen a ship from the Maxima Shipyards and appeared to be heading out of Federation space. Because the Clan was heading away from the *Fermi*'s location, Capt. Aziz was not informed until her shift began six hours later. *It's a good thing I'm supposed to hear from Lt. Nandi psychically. Otherwise, I might be too late to help him.*

The *Hellfire* was only ninety minutes away from the Typhon Expanse. As hoped, the trip from the Maxima Shipyards had been uneventful. Then suddenly, Zitag'dur said loudly "Captain, long-range sensors have picked up a Federation vessel headed toward us at high warp."

"Lucy, calculate the minimum speed we need to maintain in order to stay ahead of that ship."

Five seconds later. "**At a speed of warp six-point-one, we should arrive at the Typhon Expanse four-point-five minutes ahead of the pursuing ship**."

"Excellent… Neer, please take us to warp six-point-one."

Winters looked surprised. "Shouldn't we just go to maximum warp and outrun it?"

"No ship this size is designed to go over warp six. What would someone monitoring us think if we hit warp nine? What we want them to see is a ship straining its engines to escape being captured." He smiled. "Besides, we need to put on a show for the Brotherhood."

"Captain, we're at warp six-point-one," said Neer.

"Good... Lucy, inform us if the pursuing ship changes its speed..."

"Captain," said Zitag'dur. "We're being hailed by the pursuing ship."

"Audio only."

"This is the Federation Starship *USS Beijing*. Drop out of warp, lower your shields and prepare to be boarded."

Jax responded through a device that distorted a person's voice. "This is the *Hellfire*. I'm sorry but your transmission is garbled. Did you say you were the Used Bacon?"

There was a long pause. Then the *Beijing* repeated the same order.

"Oooh, that's what you said. I thought that was a strange name for a ship" replied Jax.

There were no further transmissions as the *Beijing* slowly closed the gap between the two ships.

Thirty minutes before the *Hellfire* reached the Typhon Expanse, Jax said: "Zitag'dur begin scanning for our Romulan friends."

Minutes later Zitag'dur replied, "I'm detecting something close to the Expanse but it's hard to tell with all the interference."

"They'll probably wait until we drop out of warp before they show themselves... Engine room, why don't you put one of those live torpedoes in the forward tube."

"Acknowledged" replied Drid.

Jax looked over at Winters. "See if she needs a hand." Winters rose and went aft to the engine room.

"You don't think the Romulans will live up to their end," asked Zitag'dur?

"It's best not to take any chances, don't you think?"

"Your reasoning is sound."

A thought crossed Jax' mind. "Lucy, when we reach the Expanse, record every change of direction this ship makes. I don't want to get in there and not find our way out."

"**Acknowledged, Captain**."

Now the fun starts thought Jax.

Two minutes before reaching the Expanse, the *Hellfire* dropped out of warp and went to full impulse power. Beijing had already slowed down knowing that it couldn't catch the smaller ship.

"Zitag'dur, where are the Romulans," asked Jax?

"There's a lot of interference but they appear to be on an intercept course and should be on top of us in one minute."

"They're cutting this a little too close if you ask me," said Jax. "Neer. On my mark go to warp one for one-half second... Zitag'dur, prepare to fire the aft torpedo once we come out of warp." Both crewmen acknowledged.

Zitag'dur began a countdown. "Thirty seconds... ten seconds... five seconds...."

The Warbird uncloaked. "Now, Neer!" The *Hellfire* was past the Warbird and within twenty seconds of entering the Expanse.

The Warbird began to change course to pursue *Hellfire*.

"Fire aft torpedo!" The torpedo left the aft tube and in less than two seconds hit the Warbird's shields. Instead of the torpedo causing an explosion, the chemicals within the torpedo began to interact with the shields and change to a rainbow of different colors totally engulfing the ship and fading in less than ten seconds. The Warbird almost came to a complete stop not knowing what to make of what had just occurred, allowing the *Hellfire* to cruise effortlessly into the Expanse.

"What was that?" asked Neer.

"Oh, that was something I've been working on for some time" replied Jax. "It's designed not to do damage but to disorient the crew of another ship... That was my first live experiment and I have to admit, it worked like a charm." He sighed. "Now all I have to do is figure out how to make the effect last longer."

"That technology has many military applications," said Zitag'dur.

Jax shrugged. "Yeah, almost anything you come up with has a military application." He caught himself. "Neer, all stop... Lucy, how far are we in the Expanse?"

"**Thirty-one kilometers**."

Drid and Winters returned to the bridge. "So now that we're in the Expanse, what do we do next," asked Drid?

"We wait."

"For how long?"

"Hopefully, the Brotherhood will think we're on their side and lead us to their hideout. Otherwise, we could be sitting here for a while."

PART TWO

Chapter 12

Being in the Expanse meant that you had neither sensors nor shields. If you were lucky, you could get a visual on a ship or object before it saw or ran into you and you could act accordingly. Just trying to maintain the *Hellfire* in its original position was a chore in itself. Lucy, the ship's AI unit, was constantly making course corrections so it could find its way out. It would be impossible for anything except a computer to be able to do this.

The waiting game had been going on for over nineteen hours and there was no reason not to think it could go on indefinitely. Jax' team were in their cramped quarters resting while he sat on the bridge waiting to act if something arose. Lucy was busy monitoring the space around them, looking for anything out of the ordinary. Unfortunately, 'ordinary' consisted of a lot of static, white noise and bright yellowish-white light.

Drid came out of her quarters and walked on to the bridge. "I can't sleep so I might as well relieve you."

"Thanks, Drid but I'd rather sit here and wait instead of lying in my quarters staring at the ceiling."

Drid was in her early-60s. Exactly, how old, she didn't really know. When she was born on Ferenginar, the Ferengi homeworld, a female's only purpose was to produce male Ferengi and teach her sons the Ferengi Rules of Acquisition. Females were not entitled to work or own property. They weren't even allowed to wear clothing, which is why you never saw Ferengi females.

Drid was an anomaly. She had owned her own business a decade before the laws on Ferenginar had changed. She had married the man of her choice, which at times she wondered if she made the right decision and she had given birth to a daughter and a son, who were equal partners in her business.

She had become a member of Section 31 almost forty years ago. She did so because she had murdered her abusive husband and had fled to avoid prosecution on her homeworld. Alone and with no friends or money she was approached by a Section 31 operative who needed someone who could infiltrate an illegal arms merchant's organization and provide Section 31 with needed intelligence. She proved to be invaluable in bringing down the merchant and was asked to become one of their operatives. Over the past decade, she had done very little field work, concentrating instead on her business.

Drid sat near Jax on the bridge. He looked at her and smiled. They had been friends and comrades for over thirty years and he had a strong emotional attachment to her, more than he had had with his wife.

"Drid, why are you here," he asked?

She looked surprised at the question. "Because we're a team."

"Yeah, I know that but you've got a business and a family and everything to live for while I only have a dead wife and an extensive resume that no one will ever read."

"Jax, you're not going to get sentimental on me, are you?" He gave her a strange look. She continued after taking a deep breath. "If it were anyone else but the people on this ship, I would be back on Vexia III watering someone's drink." Jax laughed.

"Jax, you know that I couldn't let you go out here alone to get yourself killed. I would regret not being there to keep you alive." She paused. "You wouldn't want me to be traumatized the rest of my life, would you?"

Jax smiled. "How could I find peace in the afterlife knowing that I did that to you?"

"Exactly. So Zitag'dur, Neer and I are here so we can all die in peace."

"Well, let's hope that we make it through this one and die at a later date."

"That is my plan. I'm hoping to tell my grandchildren about this adventure."

Jax stared at her with a devilish look. "You do know this is classified?"

"True, but who would ever believe it."

"Good point."

They continued to chat for some time when Lucy interrupted. "**Captain, I am picking up an object, possibly a spacecraft close to us**."

"Can you give us a visual?"

"**I am attempting to comply**."

The viewscreen came on and what appeared to be a craft slightly larger than the *Hellfire* was slowly coming into view.

"Lucy, wake the others" ordered Jax.

In less than thirty seconds, the whole team had assembled on the bridge. As soon as Zitag'dur sat at Tactical, Jax said: "Zitag'dur point a phaser at that thing, just in case."

"Captain, I'm unable to lock on but if it stays on its present course, I should be able to hit it."

"Let's hope it's friendly."

The visual of the ship faded in and out on the viewscreen. Finally, it was within meters of the *Hellfire*. "Stand down, Zitag'dur. If they meant us harm, they would have done something by now" said Jax. Zitag'dur eased his hands away from the weapon's systems.

Jax continued. "Now that it's here, what is it going to do?"

He didn't have long to wait. Without warning the crew heard a loud clang and a slight vibration against the *Hellfire*'s hull. "Lucy, analyze."

"**It appears that a large magnetic device has been attached to the outer hull for some unknown purpose**" Lucy replied. The purpose was revealed seconds later when there was a jerk felt on the ship throwing anyone standing up off-balance.

"Now that, I wasn't expecting," said Jax.

"Captain, should we try and break free," asked Zitag'dur?

"And then what?" replied Jax. "No. Whoever it is, knows where they are going and it would be rude not to accept their invitation."

Chapter 13

Two and a half hours had passed since the mystery ship had begun towing the *Hellfire*. Now suddenly, both ships came to a halt. "Lucy, has our guide been taking us on a direct route to wherever we are?" asked Jax.

"**Negative, Captain**" replied Lucy. "**It appears that the ship may have used a zigzag course to confuse us but I have extrapolated the shortest way back to our original destination**."

Jax grinned. "Lucy, that's why I still love you."

"**Your response is illogical but it is appreciated**."

Jax looked at Winters. "What can I say? She's crazy about me too." Winters stared at him blankly.

Seconds later, a large voice resonated from the outer hull and through the spacecraft. "You inside. Start your engines and make sure your viewscreen is on. Then proceed forward using only your thrusters. The static will lessen and you will begin to see a planet. Follow directly behind us to the planet's surface. If you vary off course, you will be destroyed immediately." With that, the tether connecting the two ships detached.

Looking at Neer, Jax said "You heard the man. Rev 'er up and thrusters ahead." Neer complied and the ship moved forward on its own.

Less than thirty seconds later the static on the viewscreen lessened and in front of them lay a small planet in empty space surrounded by the light of the Expanse. The best way to describe it is that it was like an egg yolk floating in an eggshell. It was an amazing sight that defied everything they had ever experienced.

"Hokey Smokes" exclaimed Jax. "Lucy, has there ever been anything like this ever recorded?"

"**Negative, Captain**."

"Well, start recording. That may be the only way the Federation will know this place exists."

Jax looked through the ship's viewscreen as they approached the planet and spoke to no one in particular "There's no other place around the place, so I reckon this must be the place. I reckon."

Winters stared at Jax. He then turned toward Drid, who rolled her eyes and replied: "You get used to it after a decade or so."

"That long, huh?"

"I'm afraid so."

The *Hellfire* followed the pirate ship down to the planet's surface and landed next to it at a large spaceport. There had to be at least one hundred ships there, most being from the same to not more than twice the size of the *Hellfire*, each probably having a crew of six to sixteen pirates.

"Jax. I think we've really underestimated the number of pirates in the Brotherhood" said Drid.

"All the more for each of us to kill" laughed Neer.

"How about we concentrate on capturing Krell first and worry about the collateral damage later" replied Jax.

"Agreed," said Zitag'dur. "But we should remind them that the Poison Clan is here and means business. After all, victory is life."

"Yes, what's the use in coming if there's not going to be any carnage" roared Neer.

Jax shook his head. "I just can't take you guys anywhere."

Before the Clan alit, Jax checked the ship's sensors which were operating perfectly. There were at least a dozen armed pirates hidden close by and ready to strike if needed. He also observed the main hatch of the ship that towed them open and five of its crewmen poured out.

"Well, I see the reception committee has assembled. Zitag'dur, you come with me... Drid, put that other live torpedo into the aft bay. If things go wrong out there do as much damage as possible. Understood?"

"Understood," the crew said in unison.

"Neer, Winters, don't come out until I tell you... Lucy, if anyone comes on this ship you don't know, defend yourself. Understood?"

"**Understood, Captain**."

"Good." Jax grabbed his holstered disruptor and strapped the belt around his waist. He then turned to Zitag'dur who was holding a pulse rifle in the order arms position and smiled. "Now, let's not keep our hosts waiting."

The hatch bay door dropped down toward the ground forming a ramp. Jax was the first to walk down. He made eye contact with the five heavily-armed and menacing looking pirates and turned their way. He could see their bodies tense not quite knowing whether to raise their weapons.

He nodded an acknowledgment to the pirates. One of the pirates who must have been the ship's captain nodded back. Jax turned his head toward the ramp and said "Okay" in a calm voice. Seconds later, Zitag'dur face became visible to the pirates. Jax studied the faces of the pirates as the swagger they had displayed seconds ago turned to fear. He wanted to smile but he knew he shouldn't.

Jax took a few more steps forward coming within five feet of the pirate captain. "Now, let's keep everything friendly. It would be a shame if things got off to a bad start."

The pirate captain looked at Jax and then at Zitag'dur. He swallowed before he spoke. "Yes, it would be unfortunate. After all, we're all friends here, aren't we?" He was a Flaxian and had difficulty smiling. A smirk was the best he could do.

"I am Saldor, captain of the *Karg* and this is my crew" he shifted his head and pointed to his crew with his chin.

"You can call me Scorpion and this friendly fellow is Zitag'dur. We are members of the Poison Clan."

Jax watched Saldor facial expression change as he tried to process what he had heard.

"I have heard of the Poison Clan. I heard you all died when the Romulans destroyed your hideout."

Jax chuckled. "Yes, and we would have stayed dead if it wasn't for the Brotherhood's increased activity." He paused. "I have to admit that what you did on Toriga IV was impressive. So much so that the Federation has been cracking down on anyone who may have had any association with the Brotherhood at any point in time... That's why we're here."

Saldor smirked, then looked at the Clan's ship. "That's an impressive ship. What's its name?"

"According to the ship's logs, it's called the *Hellfire*."

"It isn't yours?"

"It is now. It was the nicest one we could steal" replied Jax with a chuckle.

"Are there others inside?"

"Yes, but they'll stay there until your armed friends in hiding come out into the open." Jax stared into his eyes and smiled. "Things are going so well. Let's keep it that way."

"Yes, of course. Uh, half now. Half when you're all off."

"I leave one on for last."

Saldor hesitated. "Agreed."

Saldor turned toward his right and made a sweeping motion with his arms. A half dozen heavily-armed pirates appeared from behind crates and ground vehicles.

Jax turned toward the *Hellfire* and made some hand signals. Ten seconds later Drid and Winters walked down the ramp holding pulse rifles pointed toward the ground. They positioned themselves at the foot of the ramp both turning outward with their backs to each other.

Saldor turned leftward and repeated the motion. The remaining pirates made themselves visible. Jax repeated his signals and Neer came down the ramp.

Jax turned to face Saldor. "So what do we do now? Go about our business or start killing each other."

Saldor raised his right arm, whirled it in a circle, dropped it and made a pushing motion toward the ground. The armed pirates lowered their weapons and began to disperse. Saldor's crew relaxed but remained vigilant. The Clan members stayed alert.

Jax took his hand away from his holstered disruptor. He wanted Saldor to feel at ease so they could talk business. What Saldor didn't know was that Jax had his derringer ready to spring into his hands at a second's notice if any deceit was detected. Saldor holstered his weapon as a sign of good faith.

"I guess I should thank you for giving us a tow here," said Jax. "Uh, wherever we are."

"You are on Talese. And don't thank me yet. Bringing you here could be the worst thing that ever happened to you. Either you have latinum to support yourself or you're in Krell's service."

Jax shook his head. "Well, we've got plenty of latinum. The problem is that the Federation didn't give us a chance to bring it with us."

"Pity. Working for Krell will take some getting used to."

Jax shook his head. "Yeah, I was afraid you were going to say something like that." He looked around the spaceport. "Man, there are a whole lot of ships here... Everyone thinks the Brotherhood is just an annoyance. Now, I see that you've become a force to be reckoned with."

Saldor smirked. "Krell's successes have brought in many new recruits. Far more than we had anticipated." He looked over Jax and his crew. "With your reputation, you would be valuable addition... That is if you aren't spies."

Jax feigned shock. "Us? Spies? I'm shocked. Shocked I tell you." Jax's face turned stern. "Somehow I get the feeling that spies don't last very long around here." He looked into the sky and only saw yellow-white light in every direction. "And besides, who is there to tell and how would you ever contact anyone on the outside?" He hesitated. "No, this is not the place I plan on committing suicide."

Saldor smirked. "You may be speaking the truth but we will assume otherwise until you prove yourself loyal."

"Fair enough" replied Jax. "Now what?"

"First, I will take you somewhere where you can, uh, how do you humans say it, unwind. Then I will report your presence to Krell. He will decide what to do with you."

"Well, can you put in a good word for me?"

"I would if I trusted you."

"You mean after all we've been through for the last three minutes, you still don't trust me?"

Saldor looked at him blankly. "Do you trust me?"

"No. But I'm beginning to like you."

That comment produced another smirk from Saldor. "I hope you are one of us. It would be unfortunate if I had to kill you."

"Just remember that I don't die easily."

"I will remember that."

Jax motioned to Neer. Neer tapped on the communication device on his wrist and the ramp began to rise.

The crew of the *Karg* and the Poison Clan began walking toward the entrance of the spaceport. As they neared the gate a putrid but familiar smell invaded their sinus cavities. Turning past a one-story building that had obstructed their view of the gate, they spotted two corpses dangling from both sides of the entrance.

Saldor slowed down and looked over at Jax, giving Jax the impression that he should be mortified by the spectacle. Jax glanced up at the pair, showing indifference.

"So, what did these two do?" asked Jax.

"Romulan spies."

Jax sniffed the air. "How long have they been up there?"

"On a planet that only has daylight, does it matter?"

"Point taken."

Jax looked back at Winters to see how he was handling the sight and smell. Fortunately, Winters had seen his share of action in the Dominion War and had probably seen worse. He smiled at Jax. Jax responded with "Remind me not to come this way for a few weeks."

Deep down Jax was thinking *I hope they weren't our Romulan contacts. If they talked, we could be walking into a trap*. He looked at Drid who had the same look on her face as he did.

They had walked silently for about ten minutes when Jax decided to ask a fairly neutral question. "Saldor, you know I have no shortage of questions to ask you, most of which you probably won't answer but I have to ask you this. We are on a planet in a void surrounded by a sea of super-heated plasma. What's controlling the atmosphere?"

Saldor smirked. "There are three atmospheric processors on this planet. They make this planet habitable."

"In my early years before I found my true calling as a criminal, I studied engineering. Assembling one atmospheric processor under these conditions must have been a challenge. But three... I really am impressed."

"Krell will be pleased you said that... Not only is he a great leader but he is also very brilliant."

Jax nodded. "I can see why he's never been caught."

Saldor came to a halt in front of a two-story building that had the distinct smell of spilled alcohol and urine seeping out of its front door.

"You will stay here until I return. If you leave this building before then, you will be considered spies and will join the other two at the spaceport. Do I make myself clear?"

"If this place has Romulan Ale, there will be no need to leave," replied Jax.

"Good. The bartender will provide you with temporary accommodations if you need to rest."

Saldor turned to leave with his crew. He quickly turned back towards Jax. "Don't forget to stay inside the building. I would hate to see you hanging from the spaceport gate."

"Thanks for reminding us. We'll be good little pirates until you get back."

Saldor turned and left with his men.

Chapter 14

Jax turned toward the building entrance and looked at the sign over the door which was written in a language that was unknown to any of the Clan. As they stood there trying to decipher the sign a Ferengi male with his Nausicaan bodyguard exited through the door. Upon seeing Drid, the Ferengi began to bargain with Jax on how much it would cost to purchase her. Drid's pulse rifle was pointed at his head so quickly that his bodyguard didn't have time to react. When he did, he began to reach for his weapon. It was too late. Jax had his pistol in his hand and was pointing it at the bodyguard's chest.

"Gentlemen, let's not get carried away. I'll make a deal with you... If you tell us what this sign says, we'll put away our weapons and forget this ever happened."

With his chance of survival nonexistent, the Ferengi said: "Its name is *Death's Door.*"

"Oh, that's such a lovely name. I wonder if they cater weddings" replied Jax. The sarcasm of the comment escaped the Ferengi.

Both Jax and Drid lowered their weapons and the bodyguard's body relaxed. The Ferengi looked at his bodyguard disappointedly. "You're supposed to be protecting me" shaking his head. "And you let a female point a weapon at me." The bodyguard looked embarrassed.

The Ferengi looked at Drid and then at Jax and smiled. "She has spunk for a female. I like that." Then he walked down the street with his bodyguard two steps behind."

"Okay, contestants. Let's see what's behind Door Number One" said Jax as they began to enter the building.

Jax couldn't decide what smelled worse, the bar or the two bodies that were dangling at the spaceport. He had been in his share of seedy establishments in his time but this one was the clear winner. Although the outside of the building couldn't have been more than 20-years old, the inside looked like it was built during Earth's Dark Ages. Dank, stifling and cringe-inducing were the sensations that Jax felt when he first stepped inside the dimly lit room. His gag reflex started to kick in as his lungs filled with what some of the patrons of this place might consider air. He, on the other hand, could think of quite a few choice words to describe what was going into his mouth. He turned behind him and looked at his crew. Drid and Winters were experiencing the same degree of discomfort as him, while Neer and Zitag'dur showed no discomfort whatsoever.

At first, the bar's patrons paid no attention to the group that had just walked in but one by one they began to take notice. It wasn't Drid or Neer or Jax or Winters who piqued their interest because their species were represented in the bar. What caused a stir was Zitag'dur. Many of these pirates had heard about what fearsome warriors the Jem'Hadar were but had never seen one up close. Jax could sense a combination of fear and awe coming from the patrons. There were other emotions but Jax had never experienced them before and couldn't interpret them.

One thing for sure, everyone in the bar had to be wondering how an aging human appeared to be in command of a crew that included a Jem'Hadar and a Nausicaan. It seemed to violate the laws of nature. Humans could be formidable opponents but commanding those two species would have been unheard of if they weren't looking at it now.

Jax scanned the bar, which was deceptively large, for a table and spotted one at the far side of the room. He pointed it out to his crew and began weaving their way through a maze of other tables. Midway there sat an individual belonging to a species that Jax was not familiar whose legs were blocking their path. He appeared to be a little taller and heavier than Jax with a deathly grayish skin tone. Jax looked down at his legs and back at his face and asked "Comfy?"

The alien couldn't interpret the word but said rather rudely "Go around." The bar became quiet. They knew something bad was about to happen.

Jax smiled. Then swiftly bent over and grabbed what appeared to be the alien's ankles, lifted them up and pulled them toward him causing the alien to become dislodged from his chair. Jax spread-eagled the alien's legs and gently applied pressure to his nether region. The alien's first instinct was to reach for his disruptor but decided against it when Jax applied a little more pressure.

At the same time, both Neer and Drid had their pulse rifles pointed at the alien's tablemates while Zitag'dur had his pulse rifle causally pointed toward the alien's head. Winters was turned away from the table eyeing the other patrons of the bar in case someone was going to attack them from behind.

The alien looked up at Jax and smiled. Then said "Human, it seems you have passed your first test. Welcome to Death's Door."

Jax released the alien's feet and let them drop to the floor. He then stuck out his outstretched hand and helped the alien from the floor. Jax was surprised that the alien took Jax' hand so readily and offered no resistance when he was being helped up. The other aliens at the table laughed and sat down like this was a normal greeting among their species. The Clan members lowered their weapons as the threat ebbed but still remained vigilant.

Finally, the alien Jax had helped up smiled at Jax and slapped the side of his arm. He then turned his chair around, sat down and began drinking with his friends as if nothing happened. Jax took one last look at them, shrugged his shoulders and motioned the Clan toward their table.

Jax sat first with his back against the wall followed by Drid, Neer, Zitag'dur and lastly Winters who sat with his back to the bar. From where they sat one could barely distinguish the species of anyone at the bar let alone identify their face because of the haze in the room. Every now and then the bar's door would open or a group of patrons would stir the haze and one could see clearly if only for a few seconds. A Ferengi waiter who looked like he had been around when the planet was formed came to serve them. "Greetings. I see you passed our initiation without having to fire a shot. Most crews try to kill them all. Your crew is much more disciplined."

Jax tried to process what he had just heard. "You mean they wanted us to kill them?"

The waiter laughed. "Their species is impervious to disruptor fire. In fact, it acts as a stimulant to them."

"Maybe I should go back and slit a throat or two... just to lift their spirits" roared Neer.

"Maybe later but only if they seem too bored" replied Jax.

"What can I get you?" asked the waiter.

"Do you have Romulan Ale?" replied Jax.

"What kind do you want? The passable or the real stuff?"

"What the difference?"

"We make the passable and we steal the real stuff from the Romulans."

"I take it the real stuff comes at a premium?"

"Everything on this planet comes at a premium, human. But for you, I'll make you a deal."

"Well, in that case, bring us the good stuff and we'll nurse it for a few hours." The waiter acknowledged the order and walked away.

A few minutes later two Dabo girls walked over to the table. Like the waiter, their best days were well behind them. "How would you good-looking devils like to buy us a drink?"

Jax looked them over and replied "Maybe later. We're waiting for someone."

The older and larger Dabo girl asked: "Well how about you come upstairs and I keep you company until your friends arrive?"

Jax smiled at her and replied, "Your invitation is most generous but unfortunately I have taken a vow of celibacy."

"A handsome human like you, celibate. How long have you been that way?"

"Oh, about three seconds after I walked into this bar."

At first, Jax thought the two Dabo girls were going to pull weapons but they decided against when Neer made a deep guttural sound they took as a threat and thought it best to make a hasty retreat.

"Jax, you do take me to the finest places," said Drid in a soft sweet voice.

“Nothing’s too good for my favorite lady.”

Seconds after the Dabo girls had left, Drid pulled out a small tricorder and scanned the table, top and bottom, and the surrounding area. When she had finished, she looked at Jax. “No, electronic devices found, Jax.”

“Good. We can talk.” He paused. “Not that it will affect our mission but I do have to wonder if those two Romulan spies on display at the spaceport have anything to do with the operative the Empire had sent to aid us.” He shook his head. “Not the best of ways to go.” He caught himself. “We’ll give it a day or two. If we don’t get contacted, we’ll assume the worst.” Everyone nodded in agreement.

“What do we do now?” asked Winters.

“We wait.”

“We seem to do a lot of that.”

“It ain’t all beaches, casinos and scantily clad females, Bunky.” Winters got the message and stopped asking dumb questions.

The waiter returned minutes later with liter-sized mugs of Romulan Ale. Jax took a few seconds to inhale the aroma of the ale and check the color. Satisfied, he took a sip. He smiled at the waiter. “I’m amazed. It’s reasonably fresh and it’s not watered down.”

The waiter replied: “Human. Look around you. These are not the type of people to water down their drinks.” He smiled. “At least until they’ve gotten drunk.”

“I think I’m going to like you,” said Jax.

“You haven’t gotten the bill yet” replied the waiter. He proceeded to give Jax the bill which was astronomical but not unexpected. Reluctantly, Jax paid him without argument. Greedily the waiter grabbed the latinum and told the Clan that he would be back later. Before he turned to leave Jax told him “Don’t think my not arguing is a sign of weakness. If you try jacking up the price on future drinks my friends and I are not going to be happy. Understand?”

The waiter looked around the table. Neer and Zitag'dur were enough to make anyone reconsider trying anything deceptive. He shivered and shakily replied "Understood."

He then looked at Drid, who for her age was a very attractive Ferengi female and smiled. Zitag'dur looked at the waiter and said in a calm, monotone voice "I was not there but I am told that she slit her first husband's throat from lobe to lobe. Even I dare not anger her."

Drid gave a devilish smile to the waiter and patted her pulse rifle. The waiter's smile faded and he took several steps backward from the table before he turned toward the bar.

"Zitag'dur, you're developing a sense of humor" joked Jax.

Deadpanned, Zitag'dur replied, "I was not joking." Everyone else laughed.

When Jax would move his head slightly to his right his peripheral vision would pick up someone or something that appeared to be staring toward their table. He didn't want to stare but curiosity got the better of him and he casually glanced over to see who it was. To his surprise, it was a Vorta. Vortas are a genetically-engineered species created by the Founders who acted as administrators, diplomats, military advisors and other functions for the Dominion. During the Dominion War, there were thousands of Vorta that mostly served as field commanders for the Jem'Hadar soldiers sent to fight the Federation, Klingons, and Romulans. To Jax' knowledge all the Founders, Vorta and Jem'Hadar were to have returned to the Gamma Quadrant at the end of the war. Or that was the story. Jax knew that was wrong because Zitag'dur was sitting next to him and it was said that there were at least three other Jem'Hadar serving as bodyguards for the uber-rich on Vexia III. Who else could afford the ketracel-white that the Jem'Hadar needed to sustain themselves? Well, they and Section 31 who, unbeknownst to the Vexians were manufacturing the substance.

Jax nudged Zitag'dur and told him about the Vorta. "If you're interested, go talk to him. Maybe he'll have something of value to tell you... Or most likely he'll tell you how the two of you are going to take control of this planet and use it as a base for the next Dominion invasion."

Zitag'dur shrugged and turned around toward the Vorta who nodded his head at him in acknowledgment. He then got up, grabbed his pulse rifle and walked toward the Vorta. To Jax, it was amusing to see so many blood-thirsty pirates scramble like chickens to get out of Zitag'dur way.

Sometime later, although time had become meaningless on a planet with no night, a very boisterous group of pirates, twelve strong, entered the bar. Jax deduced that they were the Alpha males on the planet because when they stood in front of two tables near the bar the groups sitting at them arose and moved elsewhere. Eight of the pirates sat at the tables. Two walked toward the rear of the room and into another room which may have been a toilet. The other two stood at the bar.

Jax could not clearly make out the leaders' face but there was something about his voice that sounded familiar. He looked at Drid whose hearing was far superior to his. Her eyes met his. "It can't be," she said. Then they heard a deep base laugh that only one person in the galaxy had. It was Gargan, someone who Jax had sworn to kill.

Chapter 15

Eleven years ago:

Jax, Drid and several other Section 31 operatives were sent to the planet Aoria to retrieve some sensitive documents stolen from a Starfleet courier. These documents could incriminate several high-ranking pro-Federation government officials on the planet so getting them quickly with the utmost discretion was paramount. Starfleet intelligence had determined that a local gang leader had stored the documents in a safety deposit box at a bank-like facility he owned as a legitimate business in the middle of the main city. No one would ever look for something that valuable in such an obvious location. Plus the local police would unwittingly be there to protect the documents in the bank.

The strike team was assembled and the plan was approved. There was only one problem; because Section 31 did not have representatives on the planet, they had to rely on local help to find someone to move them through the city and coordinate the logistics of safehouse locations and vehicle transfers.

Jax had worked with Brolmin, their Aorian contact, once before and was extremely skeptical when he suggested using a Xepolite named Gargan. Brolmin assured Jax that the Xepolite was reliable and as long as you paid him and got him safely off the planet, things would be fine.

Jax' experience with Xepolites had never been good. They were good at what they did but they would shoot you in the back if a better offer came along. Jax would have preferred someone else but there wasn't anyone and time was of the essence. Things went bad quickly.

As things played out:

- Drid had circumvented the security systems so the police and gang leader wouldn't be alerted.
- Jax and Drid went in first. Jax was cosmetically altered to look like an Aorian aristocrat, Drid wore a shawl like many

of the indentured Ferengi females working for the elite. Their clothing was coated with the DNA of two recently-deceased Aorians whose deaths had not yet been reported that Brolmin was able to secure.

- Once inside Drid triggered a device she had in a bag that emitted a sonic wave that rendered everyone in the bank unconscious.
- On Jax signal, an official-looking vehicle pulled up in front of the bank and two Section 31 assets dressed as guards got out and entered. A third guard stood by the vehicle while the Xepolite driver stayed in the vehicle.
- Jax and Drid went into the vault, identified and opened the safety deposit box containing the sensitive documents. Other safety deposit boxes were opened to make it look like the thieves were after other valuables. At the same time, the two 'guards' were filling a trolley with bars of latinum. This was done to give the appearance of a robbery for the latinum first and the safety deposit boxes second.
- Jax, Drid and the Section 31 guards rolled the trolley with the latinum to the front of the bank, one came out with his disruptor drawn. The guard at the vehicle also drew his disruptor as one would expect if latinum was being transferred. There were people on the street who had seen this happen before and paid little attention.
- After the latinum was loading into the vehicle, the three guards began to get into the vehicle, one in the front seat and the other two in the back. That's when Gargan produced a disruptor and shot the front seat guard and then the two backseat guards. The front seat guard was seriously injured but managed to stumble out of the vehicle and fall to the sidewalk. Gargan fired at him a second time while he lay on the sidewalk as pedestrians scurried to get out of the way.
- Jax and Drid could see what was taking place outside but could do nothing because innocent civilians on the street

might get injured. They had to wait until the vehicle pulled off.

- As soon as the vehicle pulled off Jax and Drid rushed out of the bank yelling "The bank has been robbed. Call the police" at the top of their lungs. Bystanders converged around the bank from every direction looking first at Jax and then at the body on the guard lying on the sidewalk. Jax and Drid slowly inched toward the guard's body and determined that he was dead.
- As more and more citizens converged on the area, Jax and Drid worked their way through the crowd continuing to draw attention to the bank and not them and eventually walked away unnoticed.

Hours later, Jax and Drid made it to the safe house holding the recovered documents. Brolmin was the only one there. He had heard of the incident and was conversing with his contacts to try and find Gargan. In spite of Drid's objections, Jax had her beamed up to a Section 31 ship orbiting the planet. Jax would stay and clean up this mess.

Over the next six days, Jax moved around the city tying up loose ends caused by Gargan's deception. With Brolmin's help, Jax got to the getaway vehicle first and was able to remove the two guards and DNA evidence.

Brolmin had been extremely helpful but Jax knew it was only a matter of time before the authorities would get to him and make him talk. He had called in too many favors and someone was going to let the authorities know.

On his last day on Aoria, Jax met with Brolmin and offered him passage off the planet. Brolmin refused, saying that this was his home and he could still be of great value to the Federation if he stayed. Jax disagreed and insisted that they leave together. When Brolmin refused the second time, Jax tied the last loose end and beamed up alone.

Brolmin was well known by the Aorian authorities as someone who was into numerous shady activities. Fortunately for Section 31, he had never been known to be involved with off-worlders.

Because of this, the authorities attributed the bank robbery to local criminal activity. No one ever suspected Section 31.

Back at Death's Door:

Jax, Drid, Neer, and Winters huddled at their table. Jax knew that they had the advantage over Gargan because he didn't know who or how many people were with Jax. It was now or never.

Neer rose from the table first appearing to stretch. This caught Zitag'dur's attention. Neer made some head movements which were understood by Zitag'dur when he nodded an acknowledgment. Neer then moved to the bar where he positioned himself near one of the pirates' tables. Drid stood and slowly moved her way toward the entrance to the bar with her pulse rifle pointing toward the ground. When she was in position, Jax slowly rose, holding his tankard of Romulan ale, and slowly began walking toward the two pirates at the bar. Winters remained at the table but placed his pulse rifle on top of it pointing toward the back room.

There was a small gap between Gargan and what may have been his first mate. As Jax approached he could hear Gargan arguing with the bartender about the tab that he seldom if ever paid. Jax wedged his way between the two pirates, firmly planted the ale tankard on the bar and brushed against Gargan. Gargan was slightly startled and looked over at Jax angrily.

"Hello, Gargan. It's been a while."

Gargan's expression went from anger to confusion to recognition to fear in less than three seconds. "Uh, Scorpion. I heard you were dead." The bartender had seen this play out before and began easing away from the two. The bar became quiet.

"I am and I've come to take you back with me."

Gargan didn't know how to respond.

Jax continued. "But before I do, I want the 1,000 bars of latinum you stole."

"Yeah, uh, it was only 500."

"That includes interest and expenses for my friend's funerals." He picked up his tankard of ale with his left hand, took a sip and placed it back on the bar. Gargan's first mate realized that things were about to get ugly and took a step back from the bar so he would have room to draw his weapon. Jax ignored him.

Gargan noticed his first mate positioning himself and also noticed that Jax didn't have a weapon visible. His courage returned. "You must have just gotten here or else you would know that I answer to no one except Krell." He turned and looked at his crew who were now paying close attention. He became emboldened. "What do you have four, five people tops, covering your back. I can kill you now if I want to."

"This is between you and me. None of your crew has to die because of you" replied Jax calmly.

Gargan was surprised with the comment. He didn't know much about the person he knew as Scorpion but he knew he was not to be taken lightly. He stood there at the bar with his hands on the counter trying to figure out the best way to get to his disruptor before Jax could react.

Jax remained calm. He slowly reached for his tankard with his right hand and took a sip. As the tankard began to leave his lips, his hand became unsteady causing him to slowly raise his left hand and grab his right wrist to steady it.

Gargan laughed with delight. "You've got a lot of nerve coming in here, threatening me when you can't even hold a tankard of ale." His crew also laughed.

Jax remained calm as he placed the tankard on the counter using both hands. When his left hand released his right wrist, the cuff on his sleeve was undone. "I don't need two hands to hold a tankard."

Gargan did not process that last bit of information quickly enough. Before he knew it Jax' right hand had grabbed Gargan's left wrist and was holding it firmly to the counter. With one swift motion, the icepick that he drew from under his right sleeve was being driven into Gargan's left hand, embedded itself into the bar's counter. Gargan screamed in pain.

As Jax began to pivot his torso to his left to face Gargan's first mate, he flicked his left wrist which triggered the spring mechanism that pushed his derringer into his hand. The first mate had gotten his disruptor halfway out of his holster when he saw Jax' derringer pointed a foot away from his face. It was the last thing he ever saw.

Jax quickly shifted his torso back to his right tucking in his outstretched right hand and at the same time stretching out his right arm. His right hand grabbed Gargan's right shoulder and began pulling Gargan's body clockwise toward him. He stopped pulling when Gargan was in front of him shielding Jax from any disruptor fire. Jax then wrapped his right arm under Gargan's neck and pointed his derringer toward Gargan's temple. In spite of the excruciating pain from his hand being pinned to the bar, Gargan heard the derringer's trigger cock. In an instant the pain was gone, only to be replaced by the thought of his imminent death.

As this was taking place Drid made herself visible to the pirates at the table nearest her and began firing. One of them ducked low and tried to blend in with the other patrons who were hiding under anything that would prevent them from being killed. As the pirate rose to run, he made the mistake of running directly toward Winters. His mistake was fatal.

At the same moment, Neer lifted his pulse rifle and began firing at the pirates at the other table killing all four before they could get off a shot.

There was only the sound of footsteps on the floor when Gargan's two remaining pirates emerged from the back room. Zitag'dur was waiting for them. As they began to raise their weapons, Zitag'dur phased from one end of the bar to the other at the blink of an eye. They never saw him coming and only knew he was there when they felt his knife slit their throats.

Eight seconds after Jax drove the icepick into Gargan's hand, his eleven-man crew lay dead. Jax moved Gargan's head around so he could see the carnage. The other bar patrons began to stir but no one fully exposed themselves.

"You should have just paid me," said Jax. "You could have avoided this."

Gargan was sweating profusely and in a great deal of pain. "Look Scorpion," he said stammering. "If you want latinum, I've got plenty of it... You can have all the latinum that belonged to my crew."

"I don't want their latinum, Gargan... In fact, I don't want your latinum... I just remember the oath I made as I unceremoniously disposed of my friends on Aoria."

Gargan became frightened, knowing that he was about to die. "Look, I'll give you anything you want... I'll put in a good word for you with Krell. Anything you want."

The patrons in the bar got to see the real Gargan. The man that they feared was really a coward. He was on the verge of crying when Jax ended it.

The weight of Gargan's slumped body pulling against his pinned hand was making the puncture of the icepick look more like a long see-through gash. When the icepick finally pulled free, Gargan slumped to the floor. Jax bent over and cleaned the icepick on Gargan's tunic. When he was satisfied with the results, he slipped it back into its sheath and secured his cuff. He then ejected the shells in his derringer and reloaded.

Turning back toward the bar his eyes searched for the bartender who was crouched down at the far end with only his eyes visible. When they made eye contact Jax said "Sorry about damaging your counter."

The bartender looked at him with amazement. "Are you kidding? In my seventy years of tending bar, I've never seen death dished out so efficiently."

"Thanks... I guess" replied Jax.

"No. No. You, my friend, bring mayhem to a whole new level... The only people dead in this room are the people you and your crew wanted dead" he beamed. "Usually, half the bystanders end up dead... and that's for something trivial like two males arguing over latinum or females or something else not worth the effort."

Sensing that the violence had abated and there was no longer a threat from anyone in the bar Jax ordered the Poison Clan to stand down. With that, the bar's patrons hesitantly began to reseat themselves trying to pretend that nothing had occurred. Some built up the nerve to go over to the tables of the dead pirates to look them over and shake their heads at the carnage. There were a few that came over and spit on some of the bodies.

"I take it Gargan wasn't very well loved around here," asked Jax looking at the bartender?

"Are you kidding? There aren't three people on this planet who wouldn't have liked to have done what you and your crew did." His smile turned to a frown. "Unfortunately, one of the three is Krell." He shook his head in disappointment. "He's really going to be angry when he finds out Gargan is dead."

"So what made Gargan so special?"

"Who knows? My guess is that besides worshipping the ground Krell walks on Gargan was willing to do all his dirty work. If Krell didn't like you, Gargan would take care of you. If Krell thought you weren't paying him his tribute, Gargan would get it out of you."

"Yep, that sounds like the Gargan I remember." Jax started to say something else but the bartender interrupted with a chuckle. "Where are my manners? They call me Blin. What do they call you and your crew?"

Blin was a short, portly male or a species Jax had never encountered. To Jax, he looked like a mix of Ferengi and Lurian. The two species' homeworlds are relatively close but to Jax knowledge, their DNA was incompatible.

"You can call me Scorpion and collectively we are called the Poison Clan." Pointing to each of his crew he said their names.

The Poison Clan you say" said Blin scratching his head. "I remember hearing about you thirty-some years ago... You were wanted on quite a few planets back then."

"True" replied Jax. "It's a shame that some of those governments haven't learned to forgive and forget."

Blin laughed. "A lot of those governments have changed hands so many times that they don't know who's a bad guy or a good guy." He paused. "Hey, didn't I hear that the Romulans killed you some years ago?"

"Also true. Unfortunately, they know I'm alive and well now so my days of being dead have come to an end." Jax looked around the room. "Oh, what about the bodies?"

"Don't worry about that. This isn't the first time we've had to clean up after a dispute... We keep what's in their pockets and you get all of their assets."

"All of their assets?" asked Jax. "You mean like their ship?"

"It's your right on this planet... However, Krell imposes a tax, so don't get excited just yet."

Jax gave it some thought. "I'll tell you what. Seeing that Gargan didn't like paying his tab, I'll reimburse you for your losses... You know, one thing I can't stand is a person who doesn't pay his bills."

This caused the bartender to laugh uncontrollably. "Scorpion. I think I'm going to like you... Oh, and drinks are always on the house for you and your crew. What'll you have? Another Romulan Ale?"

Jax looked in his tankard which was still a third full. "Thanks but one tankard is my limit. Maybe my crew wants more." Neer was the only one who wanted seconds and thirds for that matter.

"Suit yourself" replied the Blin.

The bar employees were just cleaning the last of the blood off the floor when Saldor entered. He was alone, carrying only a disruptor in a holster. He looked down at the wet floor which still had small swirls of blood on it. He took a whiff of the air and smelled death. He looked over at the bar and spotted Blin deep in conversation with a Breen. He walked directly toward Blin ignoring everyone else. He said a few words to the Breen who took a few steps to his right, turned toward the bar and began nursing his drink.

Jax had seen Saldor come in and thought nothing of it when he walked directly toward Blin. What he did find interesting was the Breen with his drink. Breen always wore helmets that would filter the air which they could breathe and refrigeration suits to keep their bodies cool. Jax became curious about the Breen wondering how he could take a sip of his drink.

He also wondered why the Breen and the Vorta were not conversing. Well, at least, not today they weren't. It may have been nothing. It may have been everything. Jax didn't know but he was curious.

Jax turned his head toward Zitag'dur. "Have you ever seen a Breen eat or drink" asked Jax?

Zitag'dur thought for a minute. "No. I have seen neither."

"Well, when you get a chance, why don't you ask your Vorta buddy about him?"

Jax redirected his attention towards the bar and noticed Saldor walking toward them with what appeared to be a somber expression.

Saldor stopped as he reached the table and said while shaking his head "You have not been on this planet for half a cycle and already you've managed to kill one of our most productive crews. Krell will not be pleased."

"I imagine he wouldn't be too thrilled seeing that he thought so highly of Gargan and all... but what happened between Gargan and me was personal and I needed to confront him then and there or else he would have found a way to shoot me in the back."

Saldor thought about what Jax had said and reluctantly replied: "You are probably correct in saying that he would have shot you in the back but Krell has the last word on this planet and Gargan was of value to him."

"I'll have to give Krell my condolences the next time I see him," said Jax.

"You had better make it sound more convincing than you do now because he is waiting to meet you and your crew."

Chapter 16

Krell's compound reminded Jax of every walled estate used by just about every villain that had appeared in late-20th/early-21st Century cinemas. Twelve-foot high outer walls, armed guards at the front gate and patrolling the inner grounds and an expensive looking but not very stylish two-story building that served as Krell's home and office. Jax began to wonder if Krell was a movie buff.

As they entered through the front gate, one of the guards demanded that they turn over their weapons. The Clan initially refused but Saldor assured them that they would be returned when they left.

"I'm not worried about when I leave. I'm worried about if I leave" said Jax cautiously.

"What happens to you is up to Krell. If he wants you dead, you will die" replied Saldor.

"That's a really comforting thought."

"It was not said to comfort you. It is only a fact that you cannot deny." He paused. "If you do not turn over your weapons you will never leave this place alive."

Jax shrugged. Knowing that this was not the time to try to capture or kill Krell, he turned to his crew and told them to disarm. Reluctantly they did. Jax removed his sidearm and gave it to the guard. He decided to keep his derringer and icepick hidden under his tunic just in case. If the guards discovered it he would feign ignorance and turn them over.

Two guards asked each crewman to raise and stretch out their arms and spread their legs to check their bodies for weapons. Jax was the first to be patted down. To his surprise, they only checked his torso, waist, and legs. Jax breathed a sigh of relief. The others were also searched with the guards finding a small knife tucked in Drid's waist.

Drid looked at the guard and sheepishly said "It's not really a weapon. I only use it to clean out my ears." The guards were not amused.

From then on in, the Clan studied every structure, window, door, step, rock, and plant in the compound. They planned on building a holographic representation of the compound once they got back to the *Hellfire*.

As they walked through the courtyard they counted the number of guards and identified their species. It seemed that Krell was fond of Nausicaans for protection. Nausicaans were an ill-tempered species who seldom missed an opportunity to get into a fight. But if you had latinum they would serve you faithfully. Krell obviously had the latinum and protected himself with the best he could buy. Groups of Nausicaans would stop and look at the Clan as they walked by, their pulse rifles at the ready. They would sneer at everyone but Neer to whom they gave a greeting in their own language.

One would expect someone who had spent the last few decades robbing, stealing and plundering to have a residence full of priceless objects: a da Vinci on the wall, a Raphael sculpture in the foyer, the original Psalms of Kretow the Bajoran poet in a display case. You know, something to show you had great wealth, which Krell supposedly had. But this was not the case. Krell's residence was Spartan at best. There were various sized shipping containers scattered throughout the ground floor with markings and languages Jax did and didn't recognize. Some of the containers were open with their contents visible as you walked by. It dawned on him that being a pirate meant that you risked your life every time you went out in the hope that you would capture a ship containing something other than stem bolts and replicator parts. From what he observed it had been some time since the Brotherhood had made a big score... *Who transports valuables without an escort nowadays* thought Jax. *Maybe that's why they've changed their tactics and are hitting larger targets now.*
One particular container caught his attention. It was from Toriga IV and it appeared to contain medical supplies. Jax bristled when

he saw it. His wife had been killed when the Brotherhood attacked that planet, the memory of that day flooding his head. Killing Krell was the reason he was here and he would get his chance in minutes.

Then reality hit him. He was not alone on this mission and his mission was not to kill Krell but to capture him and destroy as much of the Brotherhood as possible. That took someone with a clear head, not someone seeking revenge.

His thoughts quickly jumped to Winters. He had seen his crewmates enter a storage building and seconds later see the building erupt in flames. Saldor was walking ahead of Jax so he quickly turned toward Winters. As expected Winters face was showing signs of rage and Jax could sense the anger in him building.

"Winters, I told you not to drink all that Romulan Ale," said Jax in a joking voice. The other Clan members looked at Winters and quickly understood what Jax was saying.

"Maybe you should drink water next time" joked Drid.

Winters realized that he too was seeking revenge instead of concentrating on the mission. He lowered his head feigning illness and said: "I'll be fine once I get the little man with the drums out of my head."

The Clan members laughed. At first, Saldor did not understand the meaning of Winters' comment but after hearing the others laugh, he deduced that it was a human expression that meant Winters was sick from drinking too much. He smirked in response causing Jax to breathe a sigh of relief.

There was a large double-door entryway just in front of them. When they got to it Saldor turned to Jax and asked him to wait. Then he knocked on the door and entered. Jax looked at the other Clan members. "I wonder how Krell is going to take Gargan's demise?"

It didn't take long to find out. From beyond the double-door, the Clan heard a loud catlike yowl followed by the sound of an object crashing against a wall. Snarling and growls ensued after that and continued for several minutes. After that, there was an eerie silence.

While the snarling was going on Drid turned to Jax and replied "I don't think he's happy... Perhaps we should come back later."

"That makes sense but we wouldn't want to disappoint our host by leaving. Would we?"

"Normally, no but this isn't going to be normal."

"True."

Seconds later Saldor opened the door and asked them to come in. As they entered the room Jax stepped on shards of a ceramic material that was once pottery but now was unrecognizable.

Jax quickly surveyed the room before turning his attention toward Krell. It too was sparsely decorated. To his right were at least a dozen small shipping crates of varying sizes. Most were open but Jax could not make out what was inside.

To his left was a table with four chairs. Seated in one of the chairs with his back against the wall was an alien whom Jax was unfamiliar. The alien was very large and at that moment seemed to be more interested in the food on the table than the five individuals that had just entered the room.

Krell sat behind a very impressive ornate desk made of some wood-like material. Standing behind him were two Nausicaan bodyguards holding pulse rifles at the ready. In spite of Nausicaans being naturally intimidating, Jax found it humorous to watch the body language of the two guards when they spied Zitag'dur. There was a slight hesitation from them as if they weren't quite sure what to do if a fight broke out. *This might come in handy when we're ready to make our move* thought Jax.

Kradik Krell was a Kzinti, who were a catlike species with orange fur, yellow eyes, pronounced fangs, ears resembling bat wings, four-fingered hands with retractable claws, and long tails. Males stood over two meters tall, with broad hunching shoulders and comparatively slender waists and limbs. Krell's orange fur was streaked with gray, indicating that he was quite old. Jax had no idea what Krell's exact age was but he remembered talk of Krell's exploits going back at least 25 years.

As a criminal Krell had carved out a reputation of being a ruthless killer as well as someone who commanded loyalty from his allies and rewarded them for their service. Jax had known that

Krell was a good leader but recent events like the raid on Toriga IV indicated that he was also a skilled tactician. What surprised Jax most about him was that he had amassed a fleet of at least 100 ships without the Federation or the Romulan Empire knowing. They had totally underestimated him.

Now here Krell was five paces ahead of him. A flick of the wrist and out would come his derringer and Krell would be dead before his bodyguards could react.

It was a great plan if he wanted to commit suicide and at the moment suicide was not a priority. Jax had brought his Poison Clan members with him and their safety was more important than ending Krell's life. There would be time for that later but for right now, finding the best way to destroy the Brotherhood was priority number one.

Krell snarled as they approached his desk. The bodyguards tensed up ready to react at a second's notice. "Tell me why I shouldn't just kill you now," asked Krell?

"Probably because you're curious" replied Jax.

"Curious? About what?"

"How a crew our age and size can come here and efficiently kill your best men."

This wasn't the answer Krell was expecting but it did make him stop and think. Finally, "Yes, yes, those were my best men. Why did you kill them?"

"We were doing a job on Aoria. It was simple, we go in, incapacitate everyone, steal what we wanted and leave. No one gets hurt and everyone's happy... Gargan decides that he wants all the latinum and starts killing some of my crew while I'm still in the bank." He paused. "I've been looking for him since then."

Krell mulled over what Jax had just said. "Aoria, you say? I remember hearing something about that... They said it was a gang war."

"I wasn't going back there to tell them they were wrong" Jax replied with a smile.

Krell almost smiled but caught himself. "They say that 1,000 bars of latinum were taken in broad daylight... I'm impressed."

"Such praise coming from you is an honor," Jax replied. "Speaking of praise, what you did on Toriga IV was totally unexpected and worked beautifully."

Krell purred. "Yes, it was beautifully executed, wasn't it?" He changed the subject. "So, why are you here?"

"Because of you."

"Me?" Krell took a defensive posture which put his bodyguards on edge.

"Yes, because of what you did on Toriga IV."

Krell rolled his head. "Explain?"

"Not only did you embarrass Starfleet, but you also killed some of their security personnel. You went from being an annoyance to someone they had to make an example of." Krell let out a low deep purr of satisfaction.

Jax continued. "Starfleet wants you bad and because of that, they are rounding up anyone who may have had dealings with you at any time."

"Things had been pretty good for us the last six years. Everyone thought the Poison Clan was dead and if we didn't do anything stupid we could live out our lives in relative comfort."

"Then you raided Toriga IV and Starfleet started digging." Jax chuckled. "If it weren't for being friends with a high-ranking government official we wouldn't have known Starfleet was looking for us." He shook his head. "I still can't figure out who sold us out."

"So what do you want from me? Revenge" asked Krell?

"Well, at the moment, we're kind of at you mercy, so revenge would mean committing suicide. And who wants to do that" replied Jax humbly.

That response was exactly what Krell wanted to hear. He had the power and having someone like the Poison Clan kowtow to him boosted his ego to new heights. He pretended that he was pondering their situation and then said "How much latinum do you have?"

"We have two lifetimes worth hidden away but we didn't have much time to get off the planet."

"No latinum, you say. Then why should I let you stay?"

Drid cut in "Oh, Captain. What about Gargan's property?"

"Oh, yeah. I almost forgot" replied Jax. "I believe there is some law here that says I get whatever he owned... and I assume that includes whatever his crew owned too, seeing that they won't be needing it anytime soon."

"Yes, yes, that is the law but I get a percentage of their belongings," said Krell with a devious grin.

"And how much would that be?" asked Jax.

A smile crossed Krell's face. "Oh, not much. Let's say his ship and you can keep all the latinum and other valuables."

Jax looked Krell in the eye. "I take it that Gargan has a really nice ship?"

Krell laughed. "You mean I have a really nice ship."

Jax smiled. "I'm sure Gargan would have wanted you to have it."

Krell laughed harder. "Maybe I won't kill you today after all."

"Well, I'm sure your bodyguards will be disappointed."

"They'll make up for it at a later date." His smile diminished and he became serious. "Human, I have many questions to ask you."

"We have plenty of time on our hands. Go ahead and ask."

Krell began by asking about his crew especially Zitag'dur. He had never seen a Jem'Hadar before but had heard about what fearsome warriors they were. He wondered how a human was able to get a Jem'Hadar to take orders from him.

Krell also asked about the ship the Clan came to the planet in. Why would a ship that size have photon torpedoes? Jax explained that from what he had read in the ship's log that this was an Arcturian science vessel that was doing research on plasma clouds. The torpedoes on the ship contained sensors, not warheads. Now that they had time Jax would try to figure out how they worked. Krell was skeptical about the explanation but let it go for now.

As they talked the alien on their left got out of his chair and began walking towards them. Jax wanted to turn his attention toward him but he was listening to Krell who might take offense if he thought you were ignoring him. Soon Jax' nose began to pick up a very strong aroma. It wasn't as bad as the bar or the two spies hanging at the spaceport but it did want to make you gag.

Finally, Krell stopped talking and turned his attention toward the alien which gave Jax and his crew the opportunity to shift their bodies and look at the being now standing within feet of them. He was a huge figure close to seven feet tall and weighed well over 400 pounds. The best way to describe his physical appearance was pig-like. He had a large head with a snout instead of a nose. On both sides of his mouth there appeared to be 1 ½" tusks which stuck out of his jaws. There was no way of knowing whether they were functional or ornamental. His eyes were dark and looked straight ahead and his pointed ears were near the top of his head. Jax could tell immediately that this species was at the top of the food chain on his planet and no doubt many others.

His body was large and his legs were relatively short and stocky. He walked upright but from an evolutionary standpoint, he still had not mastered being bipedal. Looking at the hands attached to his long arms, Jax knew that his assumption was correct. There were four digits on each hand, three fingers and an opposable thumb. The knuckles on each hand were heavily calloused and were at least an inch thick. Jax surmised that he may be still using both hands and feet for running using his knuckles to grip the ground.

Boy, I'd hate to get punched by this monster thought Jax as he finished assessing the alien.

The alien finished assessing the Clan members and turned his attention towards Jax. "So, you are a human?"

"That I am" replied Jax with a smile.

"I have heard about your species." He looked over Jax. "You do not look like a formidable opponent."

"Other species have said the same thing and found out that looks can be deceiving."

"Hmmm. You wouldn't happen to be..."

Krell interrupted. "No. These are not the ones you seek."

"Oh, are you looking for any human in particular" asked Jax?

Krell interjected himself again. "That is of no importance to you."

"As you wish" replied Jax.

The alien looked over Jax one last time, turned and walked back to the table in the corner.

Krell continued to be fascinated with Zitag'dur. He like many others In the Beta Quadrant had never seen a Jem'Hadar but knew them only by reputation. "If I had a hundred of you, I would have the most feared name in the Beta Quadrant" Krell told Zitag'dur.

"I have heard that you already have the most feared name in both quadrants" replied Zitag'dur.

Krell smiled at Zitag'dur and then turned to Jax. "I didn't know flattery was a Jem'Hadar trait?"

"He's a fast learner" replied Jax.

"Yes. Yes, of course," Krell said with a smile.

Krell asked them a few more questions and warned them about making trouble. Then he told them that he would send for them when he had a job for them.

As they left the compound, Jax said: "Real friendly fellow, wouldn't you say?"

"I was wondering if you were going to kill him," said Drid.

"In due time, my dear. In due time." He took a deep breath and exhaled. "I never thought I'd appreciate breathing this air." He shook his head and laughed. "This is the first planet I've ever been on where there is a contest to see what has the worst smell."

"I hope we've met the top three finalists because I don't think my nose can take anything worse" replied Winters. Jax and Drid laughed.

"What next, Captain?" asked Drid.

"First we find out what we inherited and then back to the ship."

Chapter 17

They spent several hours doing an inventory of Gargan and his crew's assets. Between them, they had slightly over 2,000 bars and 500 bricks of gold-pressed latinum, a tidy sum of money but not as much as one would expect from someone who had spent nearly a decade robbing ships and taking their cargo.

"It looks like being a pirate is a bit overrated if you ask me," said Jax to no one in particular. He then turned to Winters. "Remember those ancient earth stories about pirates living on wooden ships that sailed the oceans and robbed and plundered smaller ships carrying treasurers from all over the world."

"I do, indeed, Captain" replied. "But that was centuries ago and nothing of value is ever transported without a heavily-armed escort."

"True but from the look of the size of the fleet that Krell is assembling, they will be able to easily overpower any escort currently being used today."

"Good thing this planet is not close to the shipping lanes or the death and destruction caused by Krell would be incalculable" added Drid.

"Also true but there are planets with valuable resources easily within range and that worries me." Jax took a deep breath. "It looks like we've come here at the right time. C'mon, we've got a lot of work to do."

They were about to walk back to the spaceport when Drid received a message from the *Hellfire* on her wrist communicator. "**Drid, Captain. Please return to the ship immediately. There has been an incident**" said Lucy the ship's AI computer.

"Lucy, can you lock on to us and beam us back to the ship?" asked Drid.

"**Affirmative**" responded Lucy.

"Good. Beam Jax and me over on my command."

Jax looked at Drid and then at the others. "You three stay here while Drid and I investigate." He looked at Drid and nodded. "Two to beam aboard" ordered Drid and seconds later, they disappeared.

When they reached the ship they saw a body lying on the floor. "How long has he been here?" asked Jax as he ran over to the body?

"**One minute eighteen seconds**" replied Lucy.

"Good. That gives us a couple of minutes... How did he get in?"

"**He beamed in.**"

Jax saw that he was a Flaxian. He patted him down for weapons or explosives. He quickly found a small but powerful explosive charge about 3"x3"x1" in the inner pocket of the Flaxian's cloak. Taking a few seconds to appraise it, he whistled. "It has a pheromonic sensor on it but fortunately he didn't have time to arm it." He handed it to Drid. "Do you think you can activate the countdown timer?"

"Yes, Captain. It shouldn't take long" replied Drid.

"Good. Set it for eight seconds." He raised his head. "Lucy, can you trace where he beamed from?"

"**Affirmative, Captain. I have the coordinates.**"

Jax pulled the front of the Flaxian's tunic with his left hand to get him to sit up. He continued to hold him until he was able to walk around him get his right arm under the Flaxian's right armpit. Jax then released his grip and place his left arm under the Flaxian's left armpit and immediately began dragging the Flaxian toward the transporter.

Seconds later Drid replied, "Timer is set, Captain."

Jax pulled the Flaxian on to the transporter. "Okay, let's send him back to whoever sent him."

Drid handed the explosive back to Jax and quickly moved to the transporter controls. Jax put the Flaxian in a sitting position where his upper body was leaning forward toward his feet. Jax held the Flaxian with his right hand and the explosive in his left. Then he said to Drid "Let me know when you've established the transporter link... Lucy, bring up the shields as soon as he is away. Hopefully, they will think it's their buddy coming back and won't react quickly." Both Lucy and Drid acknowledged.

When Drid said "I've got a lock" Jax lifted the Flaxian slightly, activated the timer and shoved the explosive into the Flaxian's lap. He then moved quickly out of the way. In less than three seconds the Flaxian disappeared from the ship.

"**Shields up, Captain**."

"Good. Now, five, four, three, two, and one..." The ground trembled and the ship shook.

"**No damage to the ship, Captain**" replied Lucy. Seconds later. "**Incoming transmission from Neer**."

"Transmit" ordered Jax.

"Captain, is what we just heard and felt have anything to do with Lucy," asked Neer?

"You ought to know that we can't do anything quietly."

Neer laughed. "Then I take it everyone's in one piece?"

"For the time being. Unfortunately, I can't say the same for whoever sent our welcoming committee." Jax paused. "Why don't we beam over our new assets and then the three of you? Then we'll find out whose ship put a crater in the tarmac."

Neer, Winters and Zitag'dur beamed on to the *Hellfire* after the latinum was placed in the ship's hold. Jax then gave them a rundown on what had transpired in the minutes since Lucy had contacted the crew.

"We are indeed fortunate that the Flaxian did not have the explosive armed before he came on board. It could have detonated as soon as you would have beamed in" said Zitag'dur.

"He's a Flaxian. They like killing from afar. Not committing suicide" replied Jax.

"Well, why didn't you just keep him and send the bomb. He may have provided us with valuable intel" asked Winters?

"Maybe. But Flaxians are known for not divulging information. If he wouldn't, what would we do with him?"

Winters looked a little confused. Drid turned to him. "What would we do with the body once we were through torturing him?"

Winters' face turned slightly pale. "No, I didn't think you were in the torture business either" responded Jax. "It doesn't bother some people but I draw the line at that... This is an ugly business but I won't lose my humanity doing it." He paused and smiled. "Okay, team. Let's go see what went 'boom'."

They walked about 600 meters before the heat and threat of more ordinance exploding forced them to come to a halt. Jax and Drid walked up to the crew of six Romulan pirates. They looked over the two Clan members like they were about to be robbed but calmed down when Jax kept his distance and just tried to get information about the explosion. From what they were told, the ship belonged to a group of Xepolites. Jax casually asked if they had anything to do with Gargan being killed earlier. The Romulan captain spat and said that he would have loved to have killed Gargan but his crew was bigger and Krell protected him. As far as he knew both the captain of the destroyed ship and Gargan were acquainted but he didn't know how well and he didn't really care.

Jax talked to a few other crews about the destroyed ship's crew and got the same response. They were Xepolites who knew Gargan and neither crew would be missed.

"It seems we may have done this planet a public service today," said Jax as they walked back to the Clan members.

The smoke was starting to lift and they could see the damage done by the explosion. The Xepolite's ship was completely destroyed. Because the explosion occurred in an air-tight confined area, the impact of the blast was restricted to the stress points of the ship like its hatch, landing struts, portholes, or anywhere on the fuselage that had been welded together like where the nacelles were attached. Jax could see the ship's hatch almost fused to the side of another ship some hundred meters from the blast. It probably would still be going if it hadn't hit that ship. The Clan walked toward the damaged ship and could see that it had been pushed some 20 meters from its original mooring because of the impact of the hatch.

The Xepolites' ship had been flipped over when the landing struts were blown off the ship and had been blown some thirty meters from its original position after the blast. You could see the three-meter deep crater caused by the force of the struts in the ground.

Debris covered a 200-meter radius. There were two ships within 30 meters of that ship and both had been heavily damaged. One had almost flipped completely over. It would have flipped completely but its port nacelle was propped against another ship's hull. Several other ships had light damage and you could see their crews busily surveying what damage they had.

"If they weren't out to slit your throat, you could almost feel sorry for their loss," Jax said in a hushed voice.

"Captain," asked Drid. "Do you think Krell will suspect us?"

"How could he? We just got here. And besides, how would we know about that crew?"

As they walked back to the *Hellfire* Drid asked: "Captain, do you think Saldor knows anything about this?"

Jax scratched his head. "No. This isn't Saldor's style. What he did earlier today, uh, or whatever day it is, is more like him."

"What about Krell?" asked Winters.

"Definitely not. Krell enjoys killing. He enjoys seeing his victim die... Bombs offer him no satisfaction."

Winters shivered. "He's not your garden party sociopath like the rest of the people on this planet then."

"No, he's special. He takes being a sociopath to a whole new level."

Chapter 18

On a planet where the sky is always bright, the need for a good chronometer is essential. After three days of sleeping whenever you were tired and eating whenever you were hungry, it became evident that the crew needed to be on a strict schedule. Even Zitag'dur, who hardly ever rested was having trouble adjusting to the monotony of eternal sunshine. The ironic thing about this was that spacefarers were used to traveling through the blackness of space for days and weeks at a time without being in the sunshine and having no problem adjusting. Now the opposite was occurring and everyone's biorhythms were out of whack. It was annoying.

Jax decided to use the Federation's Standard Time, a 24-hour day which they would refer to as a *cycle* because everyone was used to it and being out of sync when you're dealing with an enemy that thrives in this environment could be deadly. Jax staggered the Clan's hours so someone would always be awake and on board the *Hellfire* just in case someone else had the idea of beaming someone or something on board.

From the time the Clan had left the spaceport on the first day they arrived, they had busied themselves with building a holographic representation of Krell's compound and all the streets and buildings adjacent to it within a 400-meter radius. This included memorizing the number of steps it took to cross the compound courtyard from the main gate to his residence, the number of guards patrolling at any given time and all the doors and windows of the ancillary buildings in the compound. They had done things similar to this before on other planets and it didn't take long to complete something they all felt comfortable with, at least on the outside of the residence. The residence's inside was another matter. There were still too many doors and stairs that hadn't been explored that left the Clan uncomfortable. It's not like they could go there unannounced and ask for a guided tour. It was also not a good idea to take off in the *Hellfire* and scan the building from orbit. With Krell having sophisticated technology to travel through a nebula and detect enemy ships from inside the nebula it was more than likely that he could shield his compound from being scanned and detect which ship was trying to do it. It was too risky. You had to assume he hadn't become a feared leader just because he enjoyed killing. Prisons were full of them. There was a great deal of intelligence between those two furry ears and that was the reason he had never been caught.

On what was the Clan's fifth cycle on the planet, Jax, Drid, and Zitag'dur were in Death's Door gathering information about the planet and its inhabitants. The Vorta was there as usual so Zitag'dur went over to talk with him. Drid was planning on sitting in the back of the room alone observing the people in the bar but the Ferengi waiter decided to keep her company and sat across from her. He was hesitant to get closer because he still wasn't sure if it was true that she had murdered her first husband. Having her pulse rifle on the table in front of her also acted as an incentive to keep his distance. Drid put up with him mainly because he did know a lot about the comings and goings of the bar and planet and was more than willing to tell her anything just to let her know how smart he was.

Blin, the bartender was a storehouse of information as one would expect from someone in his position. He confirmed what Jax had thought about each species measuring time differently.

"All these species from all their planets? How else are they going to keep themselves sane" replied Blin?

Jax and Blin had become friends, with 'friends' being a relative term. It's not that either trusted the other. This was a planet run by a pirate for pirates. Trust was as rare as nightfall here but after Jax had reimbursed Blin nine bars of latinum to pay for Gargan's bar tab Blin couldn't have been nicer to him.

Death's Door was not the only bar on Talese but it seemed that Blin knew everything that was going on in all the other ones. Jax was surprised that Blin just happened to mention that the Xepolites whose ship had been destroyed a few days earlier had been talking to a Flaxian assassin hours before the explosion. Blin got close to Jax and asked "Rumor has it that they were talking about you and your crew. You wouldn't happen to know anything about it, would you?"

"Xepolites and Flaxians meet in another bar hours after we land on a planet we didn't know existed and you're asking me if I know who blew up their ship," asked Jax.

"Scorpion, this is a planet where there are no coincidences. There are only moves and counter-moves," replied Blin. "And I see a counter-move." He paused for a second. "And if it was a counter-move, it was as impressive as when you took care of Gargan."

"Thanks... I think. And that's only if I did do the counter-move, which I know nothing about."

"If you know nothing, why does your ship keep its shields up all the time?"

"Good point."

Blin smiled. "Human, I think we're going to get along... Oh, and I don't think anyone on this planet will dare challenge you or your crew from now on."

"That's nice to know. We've got no shortage of governments wanting our heads on the outside of the Expanse. No use adding to that list here."

Blin reached under the counter and retrieved an old bottle. He opened it and poured out a bright-green syrupy liquid. "I only give this to my best customers."

Jax took the glass, raised it to his nose and gave it a sniff. His eyebrows raised. Amazingly it smelled a little like spearmint. He put a small bit of it in his mouth and swirled it around. It tasted like spearmint. He swallowed. It was warm, sweet and smooth going down. Three seconds later the alcohol kicked in. "WHAAOOOOH! That stuff will clear out your sinuses!" exclaimed Jax as he broke into a sweat.

Blin roared with laughter. "See human, I knew you would like it."

Jax slammed the glass on the bar. "I think all the hair on my chest just fell off," he said panting heavily. "Where did you get this stuff?"

"I've had it for years. One of the crews got it off a freighter headed for the Terran Sector. Humans will drink anything with alcohol in it so I got it cheap. The trouble is that we don't get many humans around here."

"Well pour me a tad bit more and save what's left for next time. I don't want to drink it all at once."

"If you did you'd probably die."

"True but what a way to go."

Jax was about to walk back to his table when he noticed the same Breen standing at the bar at the same spot and appeared to have the same drink in his hands. Jax turned back to Blin. "What's with the Breen?"

"Oh, him. He came in several days before you arrived. His ship was heavily damaged with most of his crew dead or dying. I think he wants to latch on to another ship. He's been in other bars doing the same thing. Why?"

"Oh, no particular reason… Like everyone else on this planet, I'm suspicious of everyone." He turned away from the bar and headed back to his table.

When Jax reached their table, the Ferengi waiter was all goo-goo eyes for Drid. That look vanished immediately when he saw Jax look at him like his death was imminent. He got up quickly, tried to smile and went about his duties.

"That guy just doesn't know how far out of his league he is," said Jax.

"He's not much but he does keep me informed of the planet's goings on" replied Drid.

A few minutes later Zitag'dur sat down at the table.

"Have any luck?" asked Jax.

"I did not" replied Zitag'dur. "He is trying to recruit for when the Founders return to the Alpha Quadrant. I reminded him that the last war did not work out well and that we have no allies…" He shook his head. "He's a zealot and is incapable of accepting facts."

"Neither the Founders nor Elvis are coming back anytime soon," said Jax with a chuckle. "What did he say about the Breen?"

"The Breen wants no part of his idea."

"Well, at least the Breen is rational." As they laughed lightly Jax noticed movement out the corner of his right eye. The Breen was coming toward them. He stood above the empty chair at the table. "May I sit and discuss business with you?"

"Why would you want to do that" asked Jax?

"Because you are the Poison Clan and I heard that the Poison Clan rocks the world."

Jax' eyebrows rose and he replied "You heard correctly. Have a seat, uh, I didn't catch the name?"

The Breen sat down. "My name is unpronounceable in your language but between us, you can call me Zhak'San. That might be easier for you to pronounce."

"That's definitely not a Breen name but it is easy to remember." He hesitated. "Oh, you can call me Scorpion and this is Drid and Zitag'dur" pointing to his crew. "Now, what's your business?"

"I'd like to purchase your ship and hire you as my crew."

Zitag'dur and Drid looked in shock. Jax' eyes widen. Then he burst into laughter. "Surely, you can't be serious?"

"I am serious... and don't call me Shirley."

Jax stopped laughing and looked back and forth to Drid and Zitag'dur, both of whom were beginning to smile. Jax broke into a smile as he looked at Zhak'San. "I thought you were part of the welcoming committee hanging from the spaceport gate."

"No. They were criminals who were promised amnesty for them and their families if they gathered information for the Empire."

"Interesting" replied Jax. "Did they ever have a chance of succeeding?"

The Breen hesitated. "Probably not but their families will be rewarded for their sacrifice."

"Let's hope their last thoughts weren't about the Empire keeping their word."

Jax changed his line of questioning. "What about the bodies and the ship you came in on?"

"We captured that ship about a week ago and put the dead and dying in stasis. Then we set it adrift outside the Expanse with the preserved bodies in it. I beamed over before the ship went into the Expanse... We hoped that they wouldn't do an autopsy on the bodies or else they would know that they had been preserved." He lowered his head. "Life is cheap here." He changed his subject. "What you did to that Xepolite and his crew was impressive. No wonder the Tal Shiar fears you."

"Let's all hope that they can put off their dislike of me until well after this mission is completed."

"Destroying Krell and his pirates is a top priority. My instructions are to aid you in any way possible."

"Good, although I'm not sure exactly how you fit into the grand scheme of things at the moment."

Jax was about to say more but the Ferengi waiter was inching his way toward them trying not to look obvious and doing a poor job of it. Jax looked at Drid. "Do you think he can hear us from there?"

"I'm not sure" replied Drid. "Let me try something." In her normal voice, she said: "I'd like to do oo-mox with that waiter. He's so virile." Both Drid and Jax looked at him for any kind of physical response but he continued to clean tables as if nothing had happened. "It should be okay," said Drid.

"Good. I'd hate to have to kill him" replied Jax while staring at the waiter. The waiter still did nothing out the ordinary. Jax turned to Drid. "I think we're good." He turned to Zhak'San. "We'll talk more tomorrow at this time." He looked around the bar and noticed a clock on the wall that was somewhat in sync with the *Hellfire*'s Universal Standard Chronometer. He pointed it out to the Breen. "There. That time tomorrow."

"Understood, Captain." He got up and said "Until then" and walked back to his spot at the bar. The three Clan members rose and walked toward the exit. Jax stopped at the bar and motioned to Blin. When he arrived Jax told him "You were right. He's looking for a ship and crew."

Blin smiled. "See you next time, Scorpion." Jax acknowledged him as they walked out of the bar.

Chapter 19

As Jax, Drid and Zitag'dur approached the *Hellfire*, Neer, and Winters were standing outside talking to two Nausicaans. They halted for a moment to assess the situation and then proceeded when they saw that the conversation appeared not to be adversarial. None the less Jax kept his left arm free in case he needed to retrieve his derringer.

When Neer saw his shipmates he turned and waved to them that it was okay. When they walked up Neer informed Jax that Krell wanted to see him now. Jax looked at Zitag'dur. "We shouldn't keep our host waiting."

They turned to leave but one of the Nausicaans said "No. Just you."

Drid was about to voice a complaint but Jax raised his hand and said "I'll be fine... but just in case you know what to do."

"Understood, Captain."

Jax made it obvious when he opened his jacket and unbuckled his holster letting the Nausicaan see that it contained his only weapon. He handed the holster to Drid, looked at the Nausicaans. "Okay, gentlemen, after you."

When they arrived at Krell's compound the guards at the gate were about to search Jax but his two escorts informed them that he carried no weapons. Jax restudied all the buildings and guard posts as he walked through the courtyard. He would compare that to the 3D model they had created to make sure it was accurate.

When they got inside the residence one of the guards knocked on the door to Krell's office and seconds later Krell bade them entry. The Nausicaan opened the door and allowed Jax to enter first. As soon as Jax entered, the door was closed behind him.

Krell sat behind his desk flanked by two guards as before. When Jax got halfway through the room Krell rose and greeted him. *That's a bit unusual.* Jax's eyes flitted around the room expecting someone to jump out from behind a crate and attack him. That didn't happen but the god-awful scent of Krell's portly guest from Jax' last visit caught his nose and made him lose his train of thought.

"Have a seat Scorpion. We need to talk business" said Krell attempting to smile.

Jax sat at one of the seats in front of the desk and got comfortable. Krell sat on the edge of his desk. His cat-like body made him look uncomfortable sitting there.

"What can I do for you?"

Krell's smile faded. "Yes… I'm told that you are an engineer."

Jax remembered telling Saldor in passing that he had an engineering background. He chuckled and said, "Well, I've studied engineering when I was younger and I try to keep up to date with new technologies but I wouldn't call myself an engineer."

Krell made a slight hiss. "Do you know anything about atmospheric processors?"

Jax scratched his head and pretended to be deep in thought. "Oh, sure. That technology hasn't changed in the last 20-30 years. Once you set them up they pretty much run themselves. All you have to do is replace a part or two every now and then… Why?"

Krell's eyes widened. "I'll get to that" replied Krell. "Can spare parts be replicated?"

"Some, yeah, if you have the right kind of replicator… Others have to be built."

Krell looked disappointed. He thought for a few seconds. "If you surveyed an atmospheric processor, could you figure out what needed to be replaced?"

"Probably… What's going on?"

Krell let out a light purr. "You've probably heard that this planet has three atmospheric processors." Jax acknowledged that he had heard. "Well, we only need two of them to provide enough oxygen for the planet and keep the other as a backup if anything goes wrong." Jax leaned forward in his seat. Krell continued. "The processors are getting older and we are using more and more spare parts."

Jax discreetly butted in. “Can I assume that you lack the necessary replicator and lack the means of getting manufactured parts here?”

“I see you catch on fast, human” replied Krell with a sinister sounding chuckle.

Jax smiled. “Catching on fast is what keeps us alive.”

Krell grinned baring his fangs. “Yes, human. It is important to stay alive.”

“Okay, if we know what we need. The question is how do we get it? I don’t think there will be any ships carrying those particular parts that will just be happening by” said Jax.

“No, but there is a mining colony half a parsec from the Expanse just inside an asteroid belt that may have everything we want.”

“Why would anyone have a mining colony this close to the Expanse? Don’t they know there are pirates in this quadrant?”

Krell laughed. “The ore mined at this colony is worthless to the Brotherhood. It is only used in construction and needs to be combined with another ore to be useful. It would be foolish to attack them and they know it.”

“Well, it sounds like they don’t know pirates very well, do they?”

“Indeed they don’t, human.”

Jax and Krell talked a few more minutes about what needed to be done on Talese and once that was done, worry about the mining colony. As Jax got up to leave, he glanced over at the corner of the room where Krell’s portly guest was sitting. He was busy consuming several different types of food and paid no attention to anything but what was in arms reach.

As he walked out the building escorted by the two guards, Jax stopped and took a deep breath, then he stretched his arms all the while surveying the courtyard. His plan was starting to take shape.

When he returned to the *Hellfire* Jax briefed his crew about his meeting with Krell. Starting with the next cycle, he and Drid would start visiting the three atmospheric processors and identify equipment and parts that need replacing. Once they have the list of parts, the Brotherhood will raid a nearby mining colony and take what's needed.

"I don't like this," said Drid. "Shouldn't they have a team that is reasonably sufficient in maintaining the processors?"

"I hear what you're saying and I totally agree with you but you have to remember, it's not easy attracting good people to work for you when you're a crazed killer... Krell kinda has to take whatever comes into the Expanse." Jax scanned his crew. "Look, I trust Krell about as much as he trusts us. I know he's up to something but I just don't know what. This is something that we're going to have to let play out." He perked up and changed the subject. "Okay, how about I close my eyes and you bring up the map of the compound and let's see if I can make it to Krell's office."

Chapter 20

Jax and Drid spent the next eight cycles inspecting the planet's three atmospheric processors. They were accompanied by Graul, a Tellarite who acted as chief engineer for all three facilities. Tellarites by nature love to argue, even when there is nothing to argue about. Graul was no different, which made Jax and Drid want to flip a coin to see who got to shoot him first.

Jax noticed that when he wasn't arguing he was purposely trying to deceive them to give them the impression that he was less capable than he actually was. Jax surmised that this may be a test on Graul's part to see if Jax had any ill intent toward the machinery or facilities.

Whether he was being deceptive or just didn't know the answer was irrelevant. There was no reason for them to lie to Graul about the facilities. They needed to function properly. And besides, they would be damaged or destroyed by the Poison Clan in the not-to-distant future if everything worked out.

Two days after the inspection, Jax, Drid, and Graul met with Krell to go over what parts and equipment were needed to ensure the long-term upkeep of the processors. Krell actual gave the impression that he was pleased with the inventory and purred loudly at the results.

"So, when do we go and get the equipment," asked Jax?

Krell stopped purring and took a deep breath. "You don't have to worry about that. I'm sending Saldor and thirty other ships to take the mining colony and retrieve all the equipment."

This news startled Jax. Part of his plan was to get outside the Expanse and inform Capt. Aziz when to come to their aid. If she didn't hear from him before they planned their escape the *Fermi* could be days away from the Expanse when the time came. He had to think fast.

"And what exactly is he going to do?"

The question caught Krell by surprise and put him into a defensive position. “And what do you mean by that” he hissed?

“Well, Saldor may be a more than competent captain and leader but he’s not an engineer” Jax replied calmly. “We have to assume that most of the parts and equipment that we need are currently hooked up to their atmospheric processors. It may take hours for us to disassemble that equipment. It’s not the sort of thing one can do using a pulse rifle or a disruptor.”

Reality hit Krell. He had a blank look on his face. Then he looked at Graul. “He speaks the truth, Krell. In some cases, several hours of work may be optimistic.”

Krell snarled loudly. He was angry that he didn’t take into account the time needed to disassemble equipment. Jax saw his weakness and decided to take advantage of it.

“We’re going to need the three of us to identify what needs to be taken and supervise when parts need to be removed from a particular piece of equipment... We’re also going to need as many ships’ mechanics as we can get. The more people use to handling delicate equipment, the better.”

Krell mulled over what he had been told. Jax continued. “My crew and I could...”

“No” interrupted Krell causing Jax to do a double-take. “What? What do you mean ‘no’?

“I mean ‘no’ because I don’t trust you and your crew yet.”

Jax thought for a second. “Yeah, I can accept that but it’s not like we can come and go as we please.”

“Not now you can’t but we would have to equip your ship with one of our transponders in order for you to navigate the Expanse... and I don’t want to do that right now.”

Jax thought quickly. “Okay... I can see that that is some technology you don’t want floating around but you said that there would be thirty other ships on this raid. That’s a lot of ships to tangle with if we tried to do something really stupid.”

Krell grinned. “Human, you have answers for everything.”

“Both of us have been doing this for a long time. Saying or doing the right thing at the right time is why we’re both alive.”

Krell grinned. “True.”

"Look, how about you put one of your engineers and a guard or two on the *Hellfire* with us? They can make sure we don't do anything out the ordinary."

Krell's paw came up to his face and he stroked his chin. "Let me think about it."

"Fair enough."

As they began to leave Krell's office Jax looked to his left and noticed that the large, pig-like alien was not sitting at his usual spot stuffing his face with different food items that didn't look edible to him. Jax wanted to ask about him but knew that Krell had no intentions of answering. He was curious to know more about the alien but in a way, he was more relieved that he didn't have to smell him today.

When Jax and Drid returned to the *Hellfire* they briefed the crew on the meeting. They decided on two objectives that needed to be taken in order to complete this mission. First, Jax needed to go outside the Expanse in order to signal the *Fermi*. Assuming they could accomplish their mission inside the Expanse they still needed the *Fermi* to cover their retreat when they escaped. If he couldn't get outside the Expanse and contact the *Fermi*, they would have to rely on the Romulans giving them safe passage to Federation space, which would probably never happen because of the history between the Empire and the Poison Clan.

Second, find a way to procure one of the transponders. If they were fortunate enough to have Krell install one of them in the *Hellfire*, even temporarily, Lucy thought she could analyze its internals and software and replicate a facsimile of it. If she couldn't she still had the route the *Hellfire* took to get to Talese in her memory banks.

Assuming that these two objectives could be met the only thing that remained outstanding was figuring out how to capture Krell which they had been working on since their first visit to Krell's compound.

Early during the following cycle, Jax received word that Krell had agreed to let the Poison Clan participate in the raid. There were several conditions attached but none that would cause the Clan any undue hardship.

"Well, team, it looks like Krell just signed the Brotherhood's death warrant," Jax said with a smile.

Later that cycle, Jax and Zitag'dur met with Zhak'San at Death's Door to brief him on their meeting with Krell. They purposely left the details vague because, quite frankly, they didn't trust the Breen. They knew nothing about him other than he knew the correct identification phrase. Krell could have gotten that out of those Romulans dangling from the front gate of the spaceport and had one of his men dress up in a Breen costume for all they knew. It was a dangerous game they were playing.

"In the next couple of days, we're going to raid a mining colony for some of their atmospheric processing equipment. We'll take you along because we're going to need to move equipment around quickly and efficiently... Any questions" asked Jax?

The Breen sat there motionless not saying anything. Jax was becoming annoyed because he couldn't read his emotions nor his facial expressions. Finally, the Breen asked "You said raid a mining colony. What happens if the miners need that equipment to survive?"

Jax could tell that whoever was under that helmet and bio-suit wasn't a Breen or even someone with a large amount of field experience or else they would have known not to ask that question. Pirates who didn't care one way or another if you lived or died were going to raid the colony and take whatever they wanted. The miners' fate had already been sealed.

"Well, let's hope they have enough ships to get them out of there before the air runs out."

The Breen thought about it and suddenly dropped his head. Seeing this Jax said, "If you don't want to come, you don't have to."

The Breen straightened up. "I will be there at the appointed time."

"Good. Now, all we need is to find out when that will be."

They talked a few more minutes and Jax told him to meet here tomorrow at the same time. If they were going to leave sooner he would need some way of contacting him. Zhak'San gave him the location of the building he was staying while his ship was being repaired.

As Jax and Zitag'dur began to leave Jax stopped at the bar to say hello to Blin who was busy at work as usual. "Don't you ever sleep" asked Jax?

"Oh, I get plenty of rest. It's not like you're in here that much."

"True but the law of averages would dictate that I would come in here and not see you at some point."

"Maybe we haven't gotten to the point yet."

Jax shrugged his shoulders. Blin continued. "Thinking about bringing on the Breen?"

"Uh, yeah. There's something going on soon and we might need him... After that? We'll see."

"Yeah. I heard about all the engineers that are needed."

Jax looked at Blin curiously. "Is there anything on this planet that you are not aware of?"

Blin smiled. "Hey, I'm a bartender. And when people drink they like to talk, even when they probably shouldn't."

With that, Jax smiled at Blin, turned and left with Zitag'dur.

The following cycle Jax and Drid attended a meeting at Krell's compound with the other ships' captains going on the mission. Saldor, who was in command of the mission briefed the other captains of their roles and responsibilities. As the briefing droned on, Jax' mind began to wander, as captain after captain talked about the number of innocent lives they had planned on taking just to satisfy their bloodlust. To them, taking the equipment was secondary. The killing was all that mattered.

When it was Jax' turn to speak, all he said was "I see that taking care of the miners have been covered, so I will stay out of your way and concentrate on taking the equipment we need and getting back here as quickly as possible."

When they returned to the *Hellfire* Jax briefed the Clan on what had transpired at the meeting. Winters' face turned pale. Jax offered him a chance to stay on Talese but he declined. Winters had seen his share of death during the Founders War. He had killed and had seen his friends die. This was going to be a slaughter and there was nothing he could do but watch. It sickened him.

Jax looked him in the eye. "I know how you're feeling because I feel the same but we've got a job to do. So save all your aggression until it's needed."

Early the next cycle, Zhak'San boarded the *Hellfire* ready for their mission to the mining colony. Already on board was one of Krell's technicians who would install and support the transponder that would enable them to navigate through the Expanse. Accompanying him were two Nausicaan guards who were there to protect Krell's interests. Jax found having them on board amusing. Krell was smart enough to know that the Nausicaans had no chance of surviving if the Poison Clan really wanted them out of the way but Krell had to give some appearance that he would have anyone or everyone killed if he thought he was being crossed.

Jax relaxed in the captain's chair daydreaming about what exactly he was going to transmit to Capt. Aziz. The Clan had talked about this the cycle before. It had to be something short repeated over and over again so the Captain was sure to understand it. It also had to be unique so she was the only person in the galaxy who would understood the message was for her.

That was the problem. Would she get the message? There had been successful experiments of transmitting psychic data over vast distances but those experiments were held in deep space far from interference like black holes or nebulae or asteroid fields. Jax would be trying it in an asteroid field as he emerged from a nebula.

Another problem was who else would receive the message. There were countless species that had psychic powers. How many of them would receive it and be able to interpret it? Were there psychics on any of these pirate ships that could figure out the message?

No pressure, man. Piece of cake.

Jax' daydreaming was interrupted by a hail from Saldor's ship checking to see if the transponder had been installed. On confirmation that it had been, the order was given to lift off and begin the trip to the mining colony.

As the *Hellfire* rose through the atmosphere, Lucy began scanning the planet's surface for weaknesses in the defenses around Krell's compound and in the larger infrastructure facilities. She also began monitoring the transmissions made by the transponder and committing its software and circuits to memory. On several occasions, Lucy was blocked by the device's defenses but was finally able to break through them by using the software the device was attempting to use to hack into Lucy's systems.

The war against the Talesian Brotherhood had begun.

For the next four hours, the only thing that appeared on the *Hellfire*'s viewscreen was a bright yellow-white light. At one point Jax ordered the viewscreen turned off because it was giving him a headache. During this time Krell's technician was at the helm following the course set by Saldor's ship as it glided through the nebula following the signals coming from the transponder beacons.

Jax marveled at how Krell was able to set up a system like this. This technology was far beyond what the Federation currently had and he wondered how Krell had obtained it. *No doubt it was stolen from some unsuspecting science team. I wonder if any of them are still alive.*

Then, suddenly, the technician said, "We're out" and Jax ordered the viewscreen turned on. There was blackness with stars and boulders, lots and lots of boulders. They had come out of the nebula into an asteroid field. The *Hellfire*'s shields came up immediately. If they hadn't the *Hellfire* would have been pelted with a destructive barrage of smaller rocks and dust that would have eventually penetrated the ship's hull.

Neer relieved the technician at the helm. It would be another two hours before they reached the mining colony and having Neer piloting the ship through the asteroid field gave Jax an increased degree of comfort.

As the technician settle in at the back of the bridge with the two Nausicaan guards Jax motioned Drid to go back and engage them in conversation. Once they were distracted Jax looked over at Winters and nodded. Winters walked over to Zitag'dur and began talking to him. Zhak'San then moved up by Neer and looked ahead at the viewscreen.

With everyone preoccupied Jax drifted into a trancelike state. Once he was ready he began to transmit his psychic message.

"Meet us at coordinates 132.0958.3 by 684.6218.5 by 264.6210.8 eight days before my birthday. Please do this for me and for me only."

Jax continued the message over and over again each time hoping that Capt. Aziz would receive it and know it was for her. If she could interpret it, she would get his birthday from the ship's personnel file and know he wanted her at the rendezvous point in nine days. If she wasn't there at that time, the Clan's chances of survival were minimal.

When he finished the transmission he thought to himself: *Well, this is why we make the big bucks.*

Chapter 21

The attack on the mining colony went like clockwork. Half of the Brotherhood's ships formed a perimeter around the colony to make sure that no ship was able to leave. Additionally, they jammed all frequencies so any transmission for help would be stopped.

Defenses for the mining colony consisted of a shield generator which had to be on all the time and some antiquated weapons systems. The miners may be armed with phasers and pulse rifles but they would be no match for heavily-armed and highly-trained pirates.

After a fifteen-minute barrage of disruptor fire, the shields collapsed and teams of pirates beamed down to the colony's surface and began eliminating any and all resistance. Fifty minutes later the pirates on the surface hailed the fleet ships to inform them that the colony was secure and the technicians could begin beaming down.

Everyone on the Hellfire except for Neer and a Nausicaan guard beamed down to the surface where they met in the transporter room with the other engineers who would strip the colony of all equipment useful to the Brotherhood. The technicians would be split into three teams with Jax, Drid, and Graul as the designated team leaders. They were in complete control of the teams reporting only to Saldor. Zitag'dur accompanied Drid on her team and Winters and Zhak'San accompanied Jax.

The first thing noticeable as Jax left the transporter room was the smell of death. It was not the familiar smell one would expect of a battlefield. There both sides were desperately struggling to defeat the other. Somehow you smell that in the air. But here, there was only the smell of anguish, of beings who were just trying to work hard and hopefully reap some lasting benefit from that work only to end up seeing someone standing in front of them with a weapon that would end their life. That smell was sickening.

As they walked farther down the corridor the first of many bodies of the miners lay on the floors ahead of them. Jax had never seen this species before. They were small, thin-framed, hairless and medium-grayish-blue. They looked as if a stiff breeze would knock them over.

Just ahead there were three pirates going through the pockets of four dead miners, seeing if they could get one last thing from them.

Jax heard what appeared to be a grunt from Zhak'San. It was hard to tell. Jax stopped and turned around to the engineers and said "The sooner we finish our job, the sooner you'll be able to find what treasure you can" with a broad smile on his face. This seemed to please the pirates because one of them yelled "Leave some of that for us" to the pirates robbing the miners. Others cheered. As Jax turned toward the front he casually looked over at Zhak'San, nudged him and said softly "Stay focused." He then looked at Winters who nodded to let Jax know that he was okay.

The warehouse was situated between the building housing the atmospheric processor machinery and the mine entrance. From there you could select what equipment you needed and easily move it through one of the two large retractable doors on both sides. Inside the warehouse was also a rack of twenty environmental suits used by miners who worked on the surface of the planetoid. Graul had suggested that they go outside and survey the equipment but that idea was quickly put aside when they realized that none of the suits were big enough for any of the pirates. Instead, Graul followed a heavily-armed group into the mine to survey equipment there.

Jax' and Drid's teams did an inventory of the equipment in the warehouse. This went a little slower than anticipated because the language on the outside of most of the crates was unrecognizable to all but one of the pirates. He had seen it before and couldn't make out most of the words but what he did know helped speed up the process. It still took Drid's team three hours to identify and beam the necessary parts up to the awaiting pirate freighter.

Jax, on the other hand, took his team to the processor building and began identifying parts that needed to be removed from various equipment. Before they began Jax informed Saldor that the atmospheric processor would be shutting down and that all other areas of the colony except the warehouse and processor buildings would be without breathable air in less than an hour.

Once the processor was shut down it became a race to remove the parts before the remaining oxygen was depleted. That would happen in about seven hours if nothing unexpected happened. In the end, three large sections were successfully separated from the processor and beamed into the hold of the awaiting freighter in less than six hours. Jax was impressed with the efficiency of the pirates working with him and wondered how people with their skills ended up killing and stealing for a living. That thought disintegrated as quickly as it appeared when he realized that this may not have been the life they had chosen but they were doing it now and because of that it was his job to eliminate them.

Jax' team was the last to beam aboard their ships. All the other teams had left the surface as soon as their tasks had completed in order to conserve as much breathable air as possible. As Jax came on the bridge he could see that his crew had a look on their faces that indicated that they were more than ready to leave this place. Seconds later, Saldor hailed the fleet and the trip back to Talese began.

There was only so much the Clan could say to each other as the Hellfire made its way through the asteroid field and into the Expanse heading back toward Talese. One of the things up for discussion was how much of the stolen equipment could be made compatible for use with Krell's equipment? "It would be a total waste of time, effort and life if none of it was," replied Jax. "I guess we'll find out when we reach Talese and start unloading."

Chapter 22

On board the USS *Fermi*, Capt. Aziz was preparing for bed after another day of watching the sun in the Ostara system imperceptibly expand before its inevitable nova. It was a once in a lifetime experience for sure but for an officer who rose quickly through the ranks because of her ability to analyze threats and provide effective solutions faster than most of her peers, sitting around watching a sun slowly expand was a bit tedious.

Two days ago three more Federation starships had arrived in the star system, each larger and better armed than the three science vessels currently there. It was a show of force on the Federation's part in the hope that the 310 vessels currently there would behave like adults. Their arrival was a welcomed relief to Capt. Aziz who along with her counterparts on the *Sagan* and *Tyson* had spent most of their waking hours resolving the many disputes, most of them petty, which had arisen among the many species and ships during the past seven weeks. Something Lt. Nandi had said months before came to mind, *'adults behaving badly'* she thought. He was referring to intellectuals who refuse to concede a point because they would have to admit they were wrong. That made her smile.

She had just rolled her prayer rug out on her living room floor preparing for her nightly prayers when her brain was suddenly bombarded with thoughts that were not of her choosing. It startled her. She had trouble trying to interpret what she was experiencing.

It took her close to a minute to realize that it may be the message she was expecting from Lt. Nandi. She wasn't sure but how could it not be. Finally, she said, "Computer, record my voice." As soon as the computer replied '**`Recording`**" she began to recite aloud any word that came to her head. She did it over and over again for several minutes even though the message seemed to be repeating itself. She decided to continue until the message stopped because she didn't know if there might be more even though it would seem unlikely.

Finally, after almost fifteen minutes the message stopped and her head cleared. She took a deep breath. "Computer, is there a variance on this message?"

"**Negative. Two sentences are repeated continuously.**"

"Repeat message slowly, five times." The computer did as asked.

She thought about the message and said "Computer, assume the numbers recited are coordinates. Generate a holographic map with coordinates." The computer complied and generated a star map of the coordinates on a device on her desk. She saw that the coordinates were just outside the Typhon Expanse. She smiled broadly.

"Computer, what is today's Earth date and what is Lt. Jackson Nandi's date of birth?" The computer complied with the request. The date of the rendezvous in the message was nine Earth days from today. The computer also told her that it would take almost five days to reach to rendezvous point if the *Fermi* was only allowed to travel at warp five.

She thought she had everything she needed but the last sentence made no sense. It seemed superfluous. Why was it in there? She had the computer repeat.

Why does it say 'for me'? For me. She laughed to herself. *Oh, Fermi.* It was Lt. Nandi's way of letting her know the message was for her. If another psychic were to intercept this message the second sentence would make no sense.

She was about to put on her uniform and contact her commanding officer when she thought *Hey, I've got three days before we leave. I don't have to do this immediately*. She stopped what she was doing, got down on her prayer rug and said her prayers. As soon as she finished she was up and heading to her closet to dress. She'd catch up on her sleep later.

It came as a rude awakening to Capt. Aziz how difficult it was when she tried to get permission to suddenly leave her current assignment in order to assist someone who was acting outside of the normal Starfleet chain of command. How does someone tell their commanding officer that she had received a psychic message hours earlier and had interpreted it as a) being sent directly to her through the vastness of space and b) asking her to be at certain coordinates almost nine standard days from now?

Actually, Capt. Aziz thought it best to leave out the part about receiving the message psychically. That could lead to questions about how she had suddenly developed psychic abilities and whom she developed this psychic link with. It was better to say that the message was encoded and hope her commanding officer would not ask for more detail.

To say that Adm. Lydia Merino, was a bit skeptical would be an understatement, especially since the mission was classified and Capt. Aziz could not tell Adm. Merino the specifics. That brought up another irksome issue: How did Capt. Aziz accept an assignment from an admiral whom she did not report directly to? Capt. Aziz could only refer her to Adm. Blaine who had Okayed this mission and who had said he would personally talk to her CO. The admiral did admit that she had talked with Adm. Blaine weeks earlier but he had been equally evasive when it came to specifics. Nothing had been requested and nothing had been resolved. Adm. Merino did say that she would contact Adm. Blaine and if he was not more forthright with his answers he would have to find someone else.

Capt. Aziz' heart dropped into her stomach. She had promised Lt. Nandi that she would be waiting for him when he emerged from the Expanse. If Adm. Merino would not allow it and Lt. Nandi was killed, she would not be able to forgive herself. Worse yet, if Lt. Nandi were to survive, how could she face him.

How do I get myself into these situations?

Seven hours later, Capt. Aziz was hailed by Adm. Merino while she was on the bridge. She decided to take it in her ready room. Once seated she brought the viewscreen up and was addressed by her CO.

"Captain, I have had a lengthy conversation with Admiral Blaine... That man with all his secrets really annoys me" she said with an exasperated look on her face. She continued. “Nonetheless, it appears that you have somehow gotten yourself involved in an unauthorized action aimed at eliminating the Talesian Brotherhood.” Capt. Aziz’ sat quietly waiting to be reprimanded or worse.

The admiral continued. “How and why you got involved he refused to answer and somehow I get the feeling that you will not answer that question even if I give you a direct order.” The captain knew she was in real trouble now.

“What he did answer was when I asked him why it was so important that you be involved. His reply was ‘Can you think of any other starship captain you would rather have to cover their escape?’” She paused. “I couldn’t come up with a name.”

She paused again. “Captain, please make arrangements with Captains Stanton and Liebowitz to transfer your science teams to their ships while you are on your mission to the Typhon Expanse.”

Capt. Aziz burst into a huge smile. “Thank you, Admiral. Thank you. I will do that immediately.”

“Captain, in the future if you are approached by any other admiral or organization within Starfleet or the Federation, I will expect you to inform me immediately... Understood?”

Her smile faded. “Yes, Admiral. Understood.”

In a subdued voice, the admiral said “Oh, and Captain. The Talesian Brotherhood doesn’t care who the captain of a Federation Starship is. Be careful.”

“Yes, Admiral. I will.”

Chapter 23

Some of the stolen machinery was compatible with the planet's atmospheric processors. Some could be jury-rigged if the need arose and some was totally worthless. Maybe those parts could be used for something else on the planet. That's the price one pays when you steal things for a living. You can't go back and exchange them or demand a refund.

It had taken them four long cycles to go through all the items taken from the mining colony to come to that conclusion. They were better off now than they were before the raid but the time and effort expended and the lives taken for this endeavor wasn't worth it. If they were going to get the parts they had to go far beyond the safety of the Expanse and risk being confronted by Federation or Romulan starships who were now patrolling the sectors adjacent to the Expanse in greater numbers.

What no one knew was the sheer size of the fleet that Krell had assembled. He had the ability to attack a smaller target with thirty ships just to draw the Federation away from a larger target and attack the larger target with even more ships. A Constellation Class starship, even with its size and firepower would eventually fall prey to a fleet that size. Krell was holding his cards close to his chest and no one knew he was holding a winning hand.

When Jax, Drid, and Graul reported their findings to Krell, he was not happy. The only time Jax had seen him more irritated was when Krell was told that the Poison Clan had killed Gargan and his entire crew. Jax was hoping that Krell wouldn't start throwing things as he had then.

The meeting ended shortly afterward and they got up to leave. Then, for no apparent reason, Krell asked Jax "So, how is your Breen working out?"

The question caught Jax off guard. He hesitated and then said, "Well, he seems to be able to follow instructions when moving boxes and equipment around but who knows what he'll do in a firefight."

Krell looked down slowly, then back up. "Do you trust him?"

Another unexpected question. "This is the first time I've worked with a Breen. My mind keeps going to that old Romulan proverb 'Never turn your back on a Breen...' Why?"

Krell shook his head "Oh, no reason in particular. He's been looking for a crew to join since he got here. Just curious."

"Well, if we use him on our next mission, we'll keep an eye on him and let you know if anything looks strange."

"You do that."

Jax was about to turn when his eyes widen. "By the way, when is our next mission?"

Krell stammered. "I don't have anything for you at the moment. You'll have to be patient."

As Jax turned to leave he caught a glimpse of Krell's fleshy and malodorous guest once again sitting in the corner eating whatever it was that he ate in great quantities. His aroma was still strong. Apparently, whomever he had come to meet still hadn't arrived and with the increased activity of Starfleet in the area, it was doubtful that anyone would ever show up.

When Jax and Drid returned to the *Hellfire* the rest of the Clan including Zhak'San were present. After briefing the crew Jax turned to Zhak'San. "You seem to be popular."

Zhak'San was unaware of why, so Jax told him the story. Jax pondered what happened. "Hmmm, you know, this may even work out better than our original plan."

The cycle before the Poison Clan would attempt to capture Krell started off with an unusual amount of activity in the spaceport. Dozens of crews were busy prepping their ships for something big. Whatever that may have been was a mystery to Jax and his crew because they had not been asked to participate. This shouldn't have bothered Jax but he liked to be in on the action and not knowing what was about to take place annoyed him.

However, he quickly broke into a smile when he realized that whatever was about to happen meant that there would be fewer ships and crews to deal with twenty-four hours from now. *We may just get a lucky break.*

Since returning from the mining colony raid Lucy had finished replicating the transponder needed to get them out of the Expanse. She had performed thousands of simulations trying to prove its reliability and had come up with an 83.6% probability of success. She would have preferred higher results but for some reason, the transponder beacon signals she had been able to receive had been sporadic and weak. She wouldn't know for sure how successfully the transponder would work until it actually received a strong, continuous signal.

"Well, let's hope they don't change the frequencies regularly. Wandering around a nebula with no shields or a way out is not going to end well for us" said Jax.

The Clan had rehearsed their plan for capturing Krell and their escape over and over again. A lot of it depended on Krell's curiosity, something that was evident each time Jax had interacted with him. He was a cold-blooded killer but he didn't appear to act without careful thought. It's probably why he had never been captured.

Jax asked Winters to accompany him to Death's Door and catch up on the gossip. There wasn't much else to do that cycle. As they entered, Blin was behind the bar, as usual, waiting on a customer. When he saw Jax he smiled and waved and proceeded to reach under the bar and retrieve that dusty bottle of spearmint flavored liquor that Jax had come to love and a tankard of Romulan ale for Winters.

"So, Scorpion, I take it you won't be on this mission or else you wouldn't be drinking that stuff?" asked Blin.

"No. I wasn't invited," replied Jax taking a small sip of his drink and wincing as it went down. "What's going on?"

"I don't know. It must be important because only the captains know and they're not telling."

Jax chuckled. "You? Not know? Then it must really be important."

Jax looked around the bar and noticed that many of the 'regulars' were missing. He figured that they were going to be part of the mission and looked back at Blin. "Hey, have you seen that Breen?"

Blin thought for a second. "Yeah, I did earlier. He was talking to Saldor. They walked out together."

Jax scratched his head. "That's strange. He was supposed to meet us an hour or so ago."

"Maybe he got a better offer?"

"Could be but it would have been nice if he had said something."

Blin laughed. "Who does anything nice around here?"

"You got me there, buddy."

Blin had other customers to attend to so he walked away leaving Jax and Winters to finished their drinks alone. When they finished, Jax scanned the bar one last time. His eyes finally fixed on Blin talking to one of his regulars. *I hope he makes it off this planet.* Jax then nodded to Winters that it was time to leave and they walked out Death's Door for the last time.

Chapter 24

The nice thing about living on a vacuum sealed spacecraft is that you can sleep peacefully no matter how much of a ruckus is going on outside. That was the case for the crew of the *Hellfire* who slept like babies as nearly one-third of Krell's fleet took off for parts unknown. Zitag'dur had been awake during this time but the fleet's departure was the least of his concerns. To him capturing Krell and destroying as many ships and crews as possible were the reason why the Jem'Hadar existed. He looked forward to the battle ahead confident that they would be victorious.

Jax appeared on the bridge looking well rested and ready for battle. He then went over to the food replicator, ordered his breakfast and began eating in the captain's chair. He was a man of many talents but he had yet to master eating food resting on his lap without dropping a good portion of it.

By now Neer, Winters, and Drid were on the bridge acting no different than they had normally acted the past few weeks. Drid looked at Jax eating something that looked like a burnt piece of flatbread. "Captain, how did your wife keep you from dirtying up your quarters?"

Sheepishly he replied, "She made me eat at the table."

Drid's eyes widened. "Your wife actually made you do that?"

"Yeah. If I hadn't she probably would have yelled at me."

That reply produced a roar of laughter from the crew. It was what they needed to break the tension that was starting to develop as the minutes began ticking down toward their date with destiny.

Drid sat down in the Communications' chair and opened a drawer near the floor. She fumbled around in it for a few seconds then smiled. "Ah, here it is." She pulled out what looked like a large metallic-cloth which may have been used as a blanket. Spinning her chair around toward Jax she said: "Here, take this."

Jax reached over to take it and his burnt bread slice began to slip out his lap. Reflexively, he grabbed the bread and then took the blanket. "What is this?"

"It is something to put on your lap while you eat so you don't get your pants and chair dirty" replied Drid as if she were talking to a five-year-old.

"Oh, yeah, I knew that."

Drid sprang to her feet. "Here. Give me this burnt stuff so you can put this cloth on your lap." She shook her head. "How did you ever become my commanding officer?"

For the next hour or so everyone had breakfast and talked about nothing in particular, occasionally joking about something and laughing heartily. Suddenly, the ship's proximity sensors caused the viewscreen to flash on revealing the same two armed Nausicaan guards that had been to the ship before heading their way. Jax was about to lower the gangplank and greet them but he hesitated. "Lucy, scan the area for other armed pirates."

Three seconds later Lucy responded, "**There are no immediate threats within a 50-meter radius**."

Jax strapped his disruptor to his waist and walked out to greet them. After several minutes of discussion, Jax turned and motioned the others to come outside. When they had assembled, Jax told them that Krell wanted to speak to them about an important matter that would be of great interest to them. The request, of course, meant going immediately so Jax had everyone take off their weapons in front of the guards and give them to Winters. Winters would place them inside the *Hellfire* and raise the gangplank when he was back with the group.

As the group walked away from the ship, the engines began firing up as if they were prepping for takeoff.

As they entered Krell's compound Jax noticed an increase in security. More so than Jax had seen before. The four security guards at the gate were about to search everyone but the two guards that had escorted the Clan from their ship waived them off and said that only Winters should be searched. Having completed that the group walked into Krell's residence where there were two additional guards standing in front of his office door.

When they entered Krell's office, the two guards entered the room with them and took positions on both sides of the double-doors and shut them. Ahead of them was Krell sitting behind his desk along with his two Nausicaan guards standing a little farther apart than they normally did. Jax surmised that it was a more defensive positioning because there were six chairs facing toward Krell. One of the chairs was occupied. It was impossible to tell who was sitting there from behind. And, as usual, Krell's fleshy and malodorous guest was in the corner of the room but this time he was paying attention to what was going to happen.

As the Clan walked forward, Krell said "Have a seat... I believe you know my other guest?"

When Jax was at a better angle he saw that it was Zhak'San seated in the far left chair. "Uh, I was wondering what happened to you." He turned toward Krell and began to sit. "So, what's this about?"

"It seems that your Breen friend here has been telling me an interesting story" replied Krell. "If he's telling the truth, you and your crew could be spending a lot of time dangling from the entrance of the spaceport."

"And what if he's not telling the truth," asked Jax?

"Well, he's going to be lonely hanging from the spaceport entrance all by himself." He hesitated and smirked. "Oh, if I don't like either of your stories, I'll hang you all just to be sure."

Jax appeared to be unfazed by Krell's threat as he turned toward the Breen and calmly said "Fair enough. Tell us your story?"

"You, human, and your crew are Federation spies," said the Breen in an accusatory tone.

Jax stared at him for a good ten seconds then turned his head toward his crew. Then he turned back to the Breen and back again at his crew with a smile on his face. Simultaneously, they all began to laugh. This caught Krell off guard probably thinking that things would get heated and someone would get injured or worse. The guards were also confused not knowing whether they should be shooting someone or laughing as well.

Jax turned back to Zhak'San. "And you have proof that we're Federation spies?"

"Yes, of course" replied the Breen. "During the Founders War, my unit was captured by a special unit of Federation soldiers that wore different uniform than the regular soldiers and had different non-Federation species fighting for it. I remember you leading that unit and that Ferengi female a member of your unit."

Jax looked at Krell. "You've heard about my history. Only you have surpassed me in planets that want me dead."

Krell nodded. "True but all those warrants could be faked."

"Over a thirty-five year period?"

Krell shrugged.

"So tell me? If you deem us as spies, what does this Breen get out of it?"

"Oh, your ship and its contents."

"And that didn't strike you as strange?"

"Human, I had asked you if you trusted him."

"Yes you did and I should have said 'No, I don't trust the worthless little petaQ.'" Jax turned to the Breen his voice getting louder. "The Romulans are right about you and your species. Never turn your back on them or trust them." He began to rise from his chair slowly. The guards began to move cautiously.

Fully erect Jax stepped in front of the Breen and reached down to him and grabbed him just below his headgear and pulled him up with his right hand cursing him as he did it. The guard closest to them moved in to separate them using his pulse rifle as a wedge. As pressure was applied to his right forearm, Jax moved his left hand to support it. That's when he produced an icepick from under his sleeve and stuck it through the guard's throat into the base of his spine. As the guard's body began to crumple, Jax grabbed his pulse rifle with his left hand and moved it behind his back into the waiting hands of Neer.

While all attention was directed toward Jax, Zhak'San and the guard getting physical, Zitag'dur phased next to the Nausicaan guard to his right and snapped his neck. He then grabbed the guards pulse rifle in one hand and spun around toward the two guards standing at the door while holding the dead guard in front of him using his other hand. The guards at the door turned their attention toward him and began to raise their weapons.

Neer spun quickly and shot the guard closest to him while Zitag'dur shot the other guard before he could get off a shot. While this was going on, Jax moved his left arm back in front of him. As he did this he flicked his wrist which caused his hidden derringer to slip into his hand. Krell was in the process of reaching for his holstered disruptor but had to rise from his chair in order to do it. He was not quick enough. Jax had his derringer pointed at Krell's head before he could lift his weapon from its holster. Jax looked at Krell, shook his head and said calmly "Small weapon. Big hole." Krell's hand relaxed as the rest of his body remained motionless.

Drid circled around Krell's desk and removed his disruptor. Then she patted him down to make sure he didn't have other weapons and had him sit back in his chair with his disruptor pointed at him. He was angry but he knew if he waited he would get his chance to kill some or all of them.

Trying his best to mimic Krell's voice, Jax yelled at the door "Guards! Get in here."

As the door began to open, Zitag'dur phased toward the door and pulled one guard past him and shot the other guard point blank in the chest. The other guard was cut down by Neer. Zitag'dur picked up the guards' weapons and tossed them to Jax and Zhak'San as they approached him. Jax moved his derringer back into its wrist holster. Zitag'dur turned and left the room to search for and eliminate anyone else in the building.

In spite of his bulk, the pig-like alien was incredibly quick and agile. He had jumped over the table he had been sitting at and came charging at Neer using his arms as front legs. The tusks which they assumed were ornamental had expanded to a length of six inches, making him an extremely dangerous being.

Neer turned toward the sound of the alien and fired as it approached striking him just above his lowered head in his shoulders. There was a loud squeal and then silence. Neer then turned his attention back to the door where Zitag'dur had just exited to search for other guards.

"Wait! He's not dead!" yelled Zhak'San still looking at the alien who had only been slightly stunned and was charging again. Neer turned to fire again but it was too late. The alien rammed into Neer, driving his tusks into Neer's stomach. Neer fell back as the alien moved forward. You could hear Neer's clothes and skin tear as he fell to the ground bleeding profusely. Even though his chest cavity was torn open, he was conscious and didn't appear in pain.

Once the shock of them seeing this wore off, Jax and Zhak'San began firing their weapons at the alien. Outside of an occasional grunt, the pulse rifles that were set to 'kill' had no effect on him. In desperation, Jax rushed the alien and smashed his pulse rifle into the alien's head. This got his attention. Jax raised his left arm and reared his hand back putting his fingers in a position that resembled a cobra preparing to strike. The alien raised his head and moved it at Jax like it was going to slash him with one of his tusks. Jax reacted first as his hand came down and grabbed the alien's eye and pulled it out of its socket.

The alien squealed in agony. His head reared straight up. Jax flicked his left wrist which released the mechanism on his derringer. Once the weapon was in Jax' hand, Jax placed the derringer into the alien's ear and fired the weapon. The alien stopped moving immediately.

Zhak'San turned to Jax. "I didn't have time to tell you that those creatures aren't affected by disruptor fire."

Jax had a stunned look on his face as Zhak'San told him about the alien. He snapped out of it immediately and looked down at Neer bleeding on the floor by them.

It was a horrible sight. The tusks had ripped him open like his skin was an open jacket. Surprisingly, Neer said, "Help me up and let's get out of here."

Jax stared at him for a few seconds. "Help you up? I can't figure out how you can even talk."

Neer looked stunned. Jax then said, "Don't you feel anything?"

Neer tried to shake his head but couldn't. "How bad is it?" he asked.

Jax didn't know how to answer. His expression told Neer that he wasn't leaving that office alive. Neer calmly said, "Leave the weapon and get out of here."

Jax looked over at Zhak'San and said "Relieve Drid" as he dropped down on one knee to hold Neer's hand.

While all the action was going on in the office, Drid had held her disruptor pointed directly at Krell's head. Krell had no doubt expected her to drop her guard at some point but she held her concentration throughout the fight. Zhak'San walked up behind her and told her he'd take over. Without looking away from Krell she said "Put that pulse rifle on stun and if he moves, shoot him... We need him alive for now."

Zhak'San reset the pulse rifle setting and pointed it at Krell. Drid turned and walked over to Neer and got down on both knees. She bent over him and kissed his forehead. "Goodbye, my friend," was all she said. Then she got up and relieved Winters who stood at the office door waiting for Zitag'dur to return. Winters also knelt by Neer and gave him a few words of comfort and respect and got up and moved toward Krell with hate in his eyes.

"Winters" barked Jax. Winters halted. "Remember our mission." Winters' tense body began to relax. He moved near Krell with his weapon at the ready.

Zitag'dur returned to the office. Drid motioned with her head toward Neer. When Zitag'dur saw him lying there he phased over to him at the blink of an eye. Neer looked up at him. "Well my friend, this is my last battle."

"Yes, that may be true but it was a glorious one." Neer smiled and closed his eyes for the last time.

Jax placed his other hand on Neer's forehead. "Goodbye, my friend. It has been an honor." He smiled at Neer and stood up. Tapping the communicator on his belt he said "Lucy, how soon can you pick us up?"

"**Four minutes, thirty seconds, Captain**" replied Lucy.

"Good. We'll be waiting."

Jax walked toward Krell who was being lifted from his chair by Winters. Krell snarled. "So, you are Federation spies?"

"No. I told you the first time we met that I was retired and because of you, I've lost everything... Maybe selling you to the highest bidder will help recoup my losses."

Krell hissed in disgust. "You know you won't make it out of this compound alive. How could you expect to get out of the nebula?"

"Don't you worry your pretty little head over those details. If we don't make it, you don't make it. It won't be the best of deaths for someone of your stature." Krell hissed again. "Tie him up with something. We need him secure before we get out of here" said Jax.

Drid opened a few of the desk drawers and found several cord pieces of varying thicknesses and lengths. Blood stains and sweat permeated from all of them. She raised them in front of her. "It looks like our host has been a little busy."

Krell began to curse Drid but Winters grabbed him by the scruff of the neck and slammed his head against the top of the desk. "We just have to keep you alive. It doesn't matter what kind of condition you're in" he replied. With his head and stomach on the desk, it was easy to bind Krell's hands behind him and secure his legs so that he had just enough slack to walk.

While he stood in front of Krell's desk reloading his derringer, Jax turned to Zitag'dur. "Status?"

"There were three guards upstairs but they are no longer a threat. Also, I checked outside and no one seems to have heard our weapons' fire."

Jax turned to Krell. "My compliments to your contractor for doing such an excellent job on soundproofing your office." Krell sneered. Jax ignored him and took a somber tone. "We have less than four minutes before our taxi arrives which is not enough time to torture him to find out how we turn off the building's force field so I guess we're going to have to go out through the front door and into the courtyard."

Krell hissed. "My guards will cut you down the minute you step outside."

"Maybe. But maybe they don't really like you and they may decide that you're not worth the effort."

Krell pondered that for a second. "My guards are loyal."

"Sure they are and we'll see just how loyal they are in the next few minutes."

Jax looked at Zitag'dur and Winters. "You two take the point and stop at the front door." They acknowledged and moved quickly out of the office. Jax and Zhak'San stood on both sides of Krell, grabbed him by his arms and awkwardly pushed him forward. Drid brought up the rear.

"**One minute Captain**" sounded Lucy's voice from Jax' communicator.

They were huddled by the front door to Krell's residence peering out the windows. From what they could see the guards were beginning to look up at the oncoming ship and get agitated. Apparently, ships were forbidden from flying near or over Krell's compound and the guards were taking a defensive posture.

Krell sneered. "Your ship will be destroyed, human."

"Does someone have a gag we can stick in his mouth?" asked Jax in an annoying voice. Drid took the butt of her pulse rifle and jabbed it into Krell's kidneys, not hard but enough to cause discomfort. Krell winced. "Each time will be progressively harder," said Drid. Krell quieted but the hate in his eyes intensified.

Guards began coming out of their barracks and into the courtyard. Some guards began uncovering weapons that had been hidden from view. These weapons were more than capable of heavily damaging *Hellfire* if its shields were down.

"Damn" exclaimed Jax! "I knew they had to be here somewhere." Krell laughed and received a harder jab to his kidneys.

Jax tapped his communicator. "Lucy, identify and destroy all heavy weapons and hostile personnel."

"**Understood, Captain.**"

Krell couldn't figure out who Jax was talking to. "So, human. You have someone else working with you."

Jax didn't want Krell to know that they had an AI unit so he just said: "Didn't I just tell you that not everyone is loyal to you." Krell began to wonder if what Jax was saying was true.

The *Hellfire* had forward and back-firing phasers which could fire at a 180-degree radius. It was designed to fight space- and air-based ships, not ground personnel.

There were three ways that the Clan could board the *Hellfire* and none of them were good. First, the *Hellfire* would have to hover close to the ground so it could beam its crew on board as soon as they were outside of the building's force field. It would have to drop its shields to do that and leave itself vulnerable to heavy weapons fire.

Second, it would have to land in the courtyard and drop its shields when its crew approached. It would also be as vulnerable as before for the ship and crew.

Third, it could hover beyond the range of the weapons and beam its crew on board but in order to do that the crew would have to be bunched together in the courtyard in order to beam them all on board at once.

Jax looked at Zitag'dur. "We have to take out as much ground fire as possible." Zitag'dur nodded. Jax turned to Drid. "When the *Hellfire* lands, make a dash for the ramp and don't stop for anyone or anything?" He hesitated. "If things don't go right, you know what to do."

Drid nodded and jabbed Krell in the kidneys. "Understood, Captain." The sneer on Krell's face faded because he knew that his fate would be determined in the next few minutes.

Jax scanned his team. "We've lost one friend today. We're not losing any more." He smiled. "See you on the *Hellfire*." He placed his hand on the door and turned to Zitag'dur. "Victory is life, my friend."

"Victory is life" Zitag'dur repeated. Jax opened the door and the two charged out.

The next few minutes could only be described as surreal. It was like watching a 20th Century Sam Peckinpah-directed western on steroids. First, the *Hellfire* began its assault by hitting the compound's heavy weapons batteries, rendering them useless in seconds. Then it hit the guard barracks and the arsenal destroying the former and heavily damaging the latter. The arsenal appeared to have a force field around it that protected it from being destroyed. It didn't matter. The force of the *Hellfire*'s phaser fire was enough to kill anything within a twenty-five-meter radius.

With the Nausicaan guards busy looking up, Jax and Zitag'dur had little trouble leaving Krell's residence unnoticed. Jax went to the left. Zitag'dur to the right. Zitag'dur had the ability to phase his body from one place to another and be on his victim before they knew what happened.

Jax lacked that skill so he relied on being what he called 'mad dog mean' in his approach to fighting. The Nausicaans were fierce fighters but so was Jax. He used any tactic he had available to him to eliminate his enemies. This was a fight to the death and Jax had every intention of winning.

After destroying the compound's heavy weaponry, the *Hellfire* had to constantly maneuver itself in order to hit its targets. The Nausicaans adapted to this and tried to stay one step ahead of it. This only lasted so long because they would inevitably end up being pushed toward either Jax or Zitag'dur who would finish them off quickly and efficiently.

Time was becoming critical because the Clan had to be off the planet before the other pirates were able to launch their ships and cut off their escape. Making what would be a decision that would not be considered logically sound, Lucy decided to land the *Hellfire* and lower its gangplank. She would keep its shields up until its crew was ready to board.

Drid peered out the residence's front door and saw the *Hellfire* begin its descent. She looked at Winters and Zhak'San. "Okay, it's time to get moving. Don't stop for anything." She looked at Krell. "If you want to live a little longer, don't try anything." Krell sneered.

As soon as the *Hellfire* alit Drid threw open the front door and the four occupants made a dash for the ship. Drid brought up the rear, firing her pulse rifle at anything that posed a threat. The Nausicaan guards slowly began to notice the group and started turning their attention and weapon's fire toward them. Jax and Zitag'dur positioned themselves so they could get the guards in a crossfire. It was successful to a point.

Lucy, seeing that there was a heavy concentration of Nausicaans firing at Drid and company lifted the *Hellfire* off the ground and rotated itself to a position where its forward phasers were pointed directly at them. There was a loud explosion that caused a heavy amount of debris to be scattered throughout the courtyard. Drid and company were knocked off their feet by the impact. Drid recovered in seconds and looked ahead to see if everyone else was okay. Winters was beginning to get to his feet trying to hold on to Krell with one hand and keeping is pulse rifle ready to kill Krell if he tried something. Drid smiled.

She then looked at Zhak'San who didn't appear to be moving. She scrambled over to him staying low in case she was fired at. Zhak'San had been hit by debris from the explosion. There was a piece of hot metal sticking through his Breen atmosphere suit. He was bleeding profusely. Drid tried to get him to his feet. He made it to his knees and then collapsed. She tried again but he pushed her away and pointed to Krell. Drid looked at him for a few seconds, touched his arm gently and scrambled over to Krell and Winters. She grabbed Krell's other arm and both she and Winters began moving toward the *Hellfire*.

Everyone left alive after the blast began to recover at approximately the same time. Weapons' fire began to be redirected at Drid and company. Jax signaled Zitag'dur to cover Drid until she got on the *Hellfire*. Then he turned his attention to Zhak'San.

Jax scanned the courtyard to see if there were other guards firing at Drid. There only appeared to be the ones that Zitag'dur had just engaged. Jax checked the power supply in his pulse rifle and seeing that it was probably enough for what he had planned made a dash for the Breen. Jax glanced over toward Drid and saw that she was following Winters and Krell up the *Hellfire*'s gangplank. He smiled knowing that whatever happened to him now didn't matter. Drid would execute Part B of their plan to destroy the Brotherhood. An energy bolt missed him by inches and he refocused.

When he got to Zhak'San he was still alive but just barely. *Strange? When did the Breen start bleeding blue blood* he thought as he saw a large amount of blood on the ground?

He shook the thought off and began to lift him. *Jeez, this guy is heavy*. While he was doing this he could hear a faint voice say "Leave me."

Still trying to get the Breen over his shoulder, Jax replied "Not today, Bunky. You're coming with me."

The distance to the *Hellfire* was not far but a sexagenarian carrying someone heavier than himself was quite a chore. On a couple of occasions, he felt energy bolts whizz by him and seriously wondered if either of them were going to make it. He wasn't far from the ship when he saw Winters run down the gangplank and begin firing at the direction of the weapons fire. Seconds later Drid ran down the gangplank pulse rifle in hand.

Jax began to stumble when he suddenly felt Zitag'dur phase next to him and lift the Breen as if he were paper and run to the ship. Jax followed close behind taking one last shot at a guard and hitting him on his left side.

Jax ran up the gangplank followed closely by Drid and Winters. Before the gangplank had even risen Jax yelled: "Lucy, get us out of here." The ship rose quickly.

"**But Captain, Where is Commander Neer?**" asked Lucy.

Jax mind cleared as he sadly replied: "He won't be coming with us."

Lucy paused as if to process the information. "**Understood, Captain. He was a brave warrior**."

"Yes, he was, Lucy. Yes, he was."

Jax sat in the captain's chair and ordered the rear viewscreen turned on. He could see the carnage at Krell's compound and then viewed the spaceport abuzz with activity. The *Hellfire* didn't have much time to escape.

Zitag'dur had moved Zhak'San down to the ship's hold where Drid could tend to him the best she could. He then came to the bridge and moved to the pilot's chair where he could pilot the ship and control the weapons systems. Winters went to the engine room to make sure the photon torpedoes were ready. For some reason, Krell was lying unconscious on the bridge floor. Everyone ignored him.

"Lock on our first target" ordered Jax.

"Locked" replied Zitag'dur.

"Fire!" The photon torpedo in the rear bay fired. Three seconds later it hit the center of the spaceport creating a 100-meter-wide crater and destroying or seriously damaging most of the ships at the spaceport tossing them like toys. Even the ships that were beginning to take off were tossed around like feathers in a breeze and slammed into buildings and other stationary objects on the ground.

Jax touched his communicator. "Winters. Load the last torpedo in the rear bay."

"Aye, Captain."

Jax looked at Zitag'dur. "Bring the ship about and lock on the second target."

Zitag'dur acknowledged. Seconds later, he replied "Locked."

"Fire!" The second photon torpedo hit the largest atmospheric processing plant on the planet. In less than a second, there was nothing left of it but a crater.

"Reposition the ship and lock on the last target."

"Locked."

"Fire." The torpedo hit the center of the second largest atmospheric processing plant but did not do as much damage as the first blast. That was because the last torpedo was one of the chemical torpedoes that Jax had designed that would cause a light show when the chemicals interacted with a ship's shields. It did not contain explosives but in this case, it did not matter. Not only did the force of the torpedo striking the ground create a ten-meter-wide crater but the blast wave from the torpedo's impact flatten anything in a 100-meter radius causing the building to implode.

"If I were them, I'd get off that planet pretty soon because what air there is isn't going to last very long," said Jax.

"**The planet will be uninhabitable in forty-three-point-six hours, Captain**" replied Lucy.

"Thanks, Lucy... Oh, assuming the transponder works as advertised, how soon will we exit the Expanse?"

"**One-hour forty-eight minutes, Captain. Otherwise two hours, twenty-two minutes.**"

Jax was about to get up and go to the ship's hold when he looked down and said: "Would someone care to explain why Krell 'the terror of two quadrants' is unconscious on my bridge?"

"**Captain,**" said Lucy. "**When he was brought on board Commander Drid asked that I take care of him. Analyzing his heartbeat and body temperature, I assessed that he was ready to attack her if she became distracted. So I decided that the best course of action was to disable him.**"

"So what happens when he wakes up?"

"**I will reassess my options at that time.**"

Jax chuckled and then tapped his communicator. "Winters? Can you help me get this carcass down to the hold?"

Winters returned to the bridge and began to lift Krell up by putting his hands under his armpits. Jax grabbed Krell's ankles and lifted that end. Two minutes later they had him in the hold propped against the stasis chamber.

Drid appeared to have stopped Zhak'San from bleeding but the metal strip was still implanted in him.

Jax walked over and asked, "How's he doing?"

"He's alive but barely. We need to put him in the stasis chamber but he won't fit with his headgear on" replied Drid.

"So let's take it off and put him in."

"Breen can't breathe our air, can they?"

"No, but have you ever seen a Breen bleed blue blood?"

Drid stared at Jax. "No. Come to think of it, I guess I haven't."

"Well, let's get this headpiece off and see what's under it."

Jax held the Breen's shoulders steady while Drid undid his headgear. Underneath it appeared the face of a relatively young Romulan-looking male, although he might have the DNA of another species in him. It was hard to tell. His skin was ashen due to loss of blood.

"Now there's something you don't see every day," said Jax, in a surprised manner. He shook his head. "Who would send a kid this young on a suicide mission?"

Drid checked the pulse on his neck. "There's not much of a heartbeat." She then placed her fingers on his forehead and lifted his eyelid with her thumb. She froze with her mouth open.

Jax noticed. "What?"

She turned to stare at Jax for a few seconds, finally replying: "You better see for yourself."

Jax leaned forward as Drid lifted Zhak'San's eyelid. Jax's head snapped back and his eyes widened. He shook his head. "Hokey Smokes! This can't be!" He looked down again and saw that the Romulan had emerald-green eyes, something that was extremely rare among Romulans.

Drid looked at Jax. "This is not good."

"It will be a lot worse if he dies... Here, let's get the rest of his getup off and put him in stasis." They quickly removed his Breen atmosphere suit and with Winters' help began to put him in the stasis chamber. They had forgotten that Krell was propped against it so when they got to it Jax used the bottom of his boot to push him out of the way.

"Sorry, Your Evilness but you keep getting in our way," said Jax with a chuckle.

When Zhak'San was tucked away in the chamber the machine was turned on and his body went into hibernation. Jax looked at Winters. "We might as well get Mr. Galactic Scourge suited up while we're at it and suit up ourselves."

Twenty minutes later, the crew settled in on the bridge. Krell, who had awakened minutes earlier, was securely fastened to one of the crew chairs with his arms wrapped around its back. It was the first time the Clan had had a chance to come down from the adrenalin high that had been experiencing for the last hour.

"Can someone tell me what that thing was that killed Neer?" asked Winters excitedly. He was still sweating profusely.

Drid shook her head. "I have never seen a wound like that. His tusks cut through Neer's chest like it was paper."

"The scary thing about it was that Neer wasn't even aware that he had been ripped open. He should have been screaming bloody murder... It was like that thing's tusks contain some type of anesthetic or something." Jax looked ahead at Zitag'dur who was manning the helm and had turned his seat to join the conversation. "Have you ever seen or heard about this species before?"

"This species is unknown to the Founders," replied Zitag'dur.

"Computer. Does the database have anything about a species like that?" Jax purposely called Lucy 'Computer' in order to prevent Krell from knowing that he had an AI unit and that they worked for the Federation.

"**There are no sentient lifeforms in my database that match that criteria**," responded the computer.

Jax spun his chair around and looked at Krell. "Hey, Fur Ball the Magnificent, who or what was your buddy?"

Krell laughed. "Fools. His kind will defeat and destroy everyone in their path. And I will be his ally and will reap the benefits of their friendship."

Jax shook his head. "Well, thanks for the editorial but that's not the answer I was looking for." He removed his disruptor from its holster and pointed it at Krell. "This is my ally, Bucko. And if you keep having these delusions of grandeur, it's going to get annoyed and make you go beddy-bye again."

Krell hissed, then looked around the bridge. "Where is your accomplice that flew the ship into my compound?"

"Oh, uh, her? We, uh, beamed her to her ship.... She will be following us out the Expanse."

"Her ship will be destroyed by my brotherhood."

"Yeah. Kind of like what your loyal guards at your compound did," replied Jax sarcastically.

You didn't have to be an empath to sense the hatred emanating from Krell. Jax ignored him and looked down at his disruptor. "We kept firing and firing and those energy bolts just bounced off of him like light off a mirror" talking to no one in particular.

"Remember that species we met the first day at Death's Door. They were like that," said Drid.

"Yeah," replied Jax "but I doubt if they could have absorbed that much energy." He paused while putting his disruptor back into its holster. "We're going to need different weapons if we ever run into those suckers again." He looked at Winters. "Why don't you and Zitag'dur take this felonious feline back down to the hold? I'm starting to regret bringing him back up to the bridge. He's kind of putting a damper on all the merriment going on."

Drid relieved Zitag'dur at the helm as he and Winters physically drug Krell down to the hold kicking and screaming obscenities in his native tongue.

Jax looked at Drid. "Sheesh, that guy is grumpy. Maybe he should take up a hobby or something."

Drid just shrugged her shoulders. "I wonder how much effort Krell is going to expend trying to figure out who flew the *Hellfire* into his compound?"

Jax smiled. "I'm sure it will eat at him not knowing who was disloyal to him."

Drid returned the smile as she turned her chair around and concentrated on the controls.

Ninety minutes into their flight through the Expanse Jax asked Lucy, "So how are we doing?"

"**I have been able to pick up the beacons but if I had not extrapolated our course coming into the Expanse, we would probably be lost**."

"That's nice but what does that mean?"

"**It means that we should be clear of the Expanse in thirty-one minutes**."

"Great. Next time I talk to the Federation President, I have to ask him to give you a raise."

“**Is that what humans call ‘sarcasm’, Captain?**”

“Lucy, you know how serious I am about everything,” replied Jax feigning shock.

“**Ha. Ha. Ha,**” said Lucy attempting to be amused.

Zitag’dur turned around from his helmsman’s chair. “Captain, do you think the *Fermi* will be there?”

“If she got the message, she’ll be there… If not, anything could happen and most of it is bad.”

Chapter 25

The *Fermi* was hiding in a debris field seven minutes, traveling at Warp 9, from the designated coordinates. They had been there for fifteen hours using only life support so the ship's energy signature could not be easily detected. Capt. Aziz would like to have gotten the ship closer but there was no other place to hide a ship of that size.

The *Fermi*'s crew was on edge. They knew they were about to go into combat but with who or why had not been explained. In fact, nothing had been explained to anyone's satisfaction, not even the ship's senior officers.

Capt. Aziz sat in her chair on the bridge. She had been there for the last ten hours. Occasionally, she would get up and walk around, do a few stretches and sit down again.

What if they aren't coming? How long do I stay? That thought was beginning to cross her mind more frequently as time wore on. She would give Lt. Nandi at least thirty-six hours before she would assume the worse. Deep down she knew she would stay longer. She just sensed that Lt. Nandi would make it out of the Expanse.

Two hours later. "Captain, there are ships coming out of the Expanse," said Lt. Lof Orora, the *Fermi*'s new security officer.

"Ships? How many?"

"Twenty-five, Captain."

She looked over at Lt. Orora. "Lieutenant, what are the ships doing?"

"They appear to be spreading out like they're waiting for something to come out of the Expanse.

Capt. Aziz closed her eyes and concentrated. Commanders Montgomery and Gintok looked at her oddly wondering if she were daydreaming.

"Captain, your orders," asked Cmdr. Montgomery?

Capt. Aziz' eyes opened. "It's not time yet. We'll continue our current course of action."

They were in a debris field. Just waiting and waiting.

"**Two minutes before we exit the Expanse**," said Lucy.

"Thanks, Lucy," said Jax. "Oh, I know you've already thought of this but could you bring up the shields and begin scanning for anything and everything as soon as we are clear?"

"**Roger, Captain**."

"Captain, what if there are only Romulan ships waiting for us," asked Winters?

"We don't have too many friends in the Empire so expect a fight."

"What if Captain Aziz intervenes?"

"If she's out there, she'll fight for us. It's the Romulans who have to decide if they want to start a galactic war."

"You have a lot of faith in someone so young," said Drid.

"Joan of Arc, Earth's greatest female warrior, took command of the French Army at the age of sixteen. She has those skills."

"Well, I guess we'll find out in about a minute."

"**Ten seconds… Five, four, three, two, one… We have exited the Expanse**" said Lucy. "**Shields are up. Beginning scan.**"

In less than five seconds, Zitag'dur said "Ships' ahead, Captain."

"How many and whose?" asked Jax.

"Twenty-five with different energy signatures."

Great. Pirates. Jax had not counted on them being part of his welcoming committee. He paused for a few seconds and asked: "Lucy, do you have any idea how they are able to communicate in this nebula?"

"**Negative, Captain. I have insufficient data**."

Under different circumstances, he would be thinking about how he could capture one of those ships and analyze its communication system but this was neither the time nor this place. Surviving was a little more important.

"All stop. We need to stall for time."

The ship slowed to a halt as Jax closed his eyes and concentrated. *"Captain Aziz. If you didn't get my first message, we will be dead in fifteen minutes. If you did, your presence right now would be greatly appreciated."*

He repeated the message two more times and opened his eyes. *I might as well concentrate on what's ahead of us.*

Jax was about to give an order but Zitag'dur interrupted. "Captain, more ships coming out of the Expanse."

"How many?"

"Five."

"Great. They've cut off our retreat."

"Captain," said Winters. "Isn't this ship capable of Warp 9?"

"Yes, it is... but if we warp out of here, that will leave thirty ships free to go anywhere and make life hell for who knows how many others."

On board the *Fermi*:

Capt. Aziz had just finished stretching in her ready room and had returned to the bridge. She froze in mid-stride and closed her eyes.

"Captain? Are you alright?" asked Cmdr. Montgomery. He received no response.

Suddenly, she opened her eyes and looked at him. "Red alert" she barked, as she sat in the captain's chair! "Helmsman take us to the designated coordinates, maximum warp." Her head turned to the right. "Mister Carter, inform Starfleet that we are engaging the Talesian Brotherhood."

On board the *Hellfire*:

"Move ahead thruster only" ordered Jax. Zitag'dur acknowledged.

"Okay, let's see who blinks first," said Jax to no one in particular. He figured that the pirates would take at least a minute to figure out what he was trying to do. After that, they would know he was only wasting time and then things would get interesting.

Sure enough, sixty-four seconds later "Captain, we're being hailed by the lead ship," said Winters sitting at the communications station.

Jax grabbed the metallic cloth blanket that was draped over the arm of his chair and wrapped it around his upper body so no one could see he was wearing an environmental suit.

"Viewscreen on, Winters."

On the viewscreen was Saldor, Krell's best captain.

Jax smiled. "Why Saldor, what a pleasant surprise. So, what do we owe this honor?"

"It seems that you have done considerable damage to Talese and many of my friends. But if you surrender and return Krell unharmed, I will promise you a swift and honorable death."

Jax feigned mulling his proposal over and then replied: "I know that you would keep your word and all but your boss is a little upset with me and might prefer that I die very slowly and painfully."

Saldor smirked. "Yes, that is true. Krell does not forgive treachery and enjoys making examples of his enemies."

"Look, I have an idea. How about if we keep Krell and go along our merry way and you get command of thirty ships equipped with capable crews... How does that sound?"

"It sounds like our current situation. Only you won't be going along your merry way. So give us Krell... alive."

"Saldor, I have to admit that I respect you for your honesty. It's a shame one of us is not going to be alive ten minutes from now."

"Yes, Scorpion. I was beginning to like you." The viewscreen went off.

"Status, Zitag'dur," asked Jax.

"Shields and weapons' systems are at 100%"

"Excellent... Winters, hail the pirate ships."

Seconds later: "They are receiving, Captain."

"This is Scorpion of the Poison Clan. If you leave now, you will live. If you stay, you will die." Jax signaled Winters to cut off the transmission.

"What was that for?" asked Winters.

"So the Romulans and the *Fermi* know we're here and which ship is ours." Jax scanned his crew. "Gentlemen and Lady, Obedience brings victory and victory is life."

"Victory is life," the Clan members said in unison.

Chapter 26

Ships are designed for different purposes; some to transport, some for speed, some for maneuverability, some to destroy planets and some to fight. The *Hellfire* was the later. It was not designed by bureaucrats trying to get the most bang for the buck. It was built for the express purpose of taking on multiple targets and destroying them. In a dogfight, it was like a rapier against a broadsword, lean and precise.

Against smaller numbers, the *Hellfire* would win hands down. But there were thirty ships to contend with. All manned by seasoned crews and commanded by Saldor who was more than formidable. As long as the *Hellfire* could outmaneuver the pirates, the fight would continue. If the *Hellfire* got boxed in, the fight was over.

Within the first minute of combat, the *Hellfire* had destroyed one ship and crippled two others. With Zitag'dur at the helm the *Hellfire* could outmaneuver its opponents and hit them before they could strike back. This kept the *Hellfire*'s shields from draining so the fight could continue. However, the other pirate ships were beginning to converge on it and limit its ability to maneuver and worst of all cut off its ability to escape.

Okay, Aziz. It's time to work your magic thought Jax as he watched his escape options fade.

With five minutes to go until the *Fermi* reached the other ships, Lt. Carter, the *Fermi*'s communication officer said "Captain, one of the ships is making a general hail. Audio only."

"Well, let's hear it" replied the captain.

The bridge heard the short transmission from someone in the Poison Clan and the transmission ended.

"Well, that bandit has a lot of nerve if he thinks he can intimidate all those ships," said Cmdr. Gintok with a smug look on his face.

Capt. Aziz chuckled. "That transmission wasn't for them. It was for us."

The bridge crew turned and stared at her most probably wondering if she was becoming unfit to lead. She ignored them. "Mister Carter, can you identify which ship that transmission came from?" He acknowledged that he could. "Good. Helmsman lock on to that ship and hopefully it will be in one piece when we get there."

The *Hellfire* was trapped. All avenues for escape had been cut off. She was taking more and more hits. The shields would fail soon and the crew would be beamed on to one of those ships and eventually die a horrible death.

With three minutes to go before the *Fermi* would arrive and the shields on the *Hellfire* were down to 30%, Jax was about to give the order to self-destruct the ship. But then, unexpectedly, a Romulan scout ship uncloaked and began to attack the pirates catching them totally off-guard. Within seconds two of the pirates' ships were destroyed and the rest were scrambling to get out of the Romulans' way and regroup.

Jax knew little about Saldor but from what he saw during the next sixty seconds or so impressed him. Saldor had managed to regroup his fleet and direct twenty of his ships to attack the Romulans and let the remaining five ships continue their attack on the *Hellfire*. No one was getting away from him that day.

The Romulan ship was smaller than the *Fermi* and possessed sufficient offensive capabilities but it would probably not be enough to destroy that many ships. It was only a matter of time before it and the *Hellfire* would be destroyed.

The *Hellfire* had room to maneuver but the shields were down to 15%. Then the *Hellfire* shuddered from a hit on its aft shields.

Jax yelled "Engine room, what was that?"

"We just lost our warp engine, Captain" replied Drid excitedly.

Damn! "Drid. You might as well come to the bridge." Seconds later she appeared on the bridge breathing heavily. Jax looked at her and smiled. She smiled back. Then he looked at Winters and Zitag'dur and said: "It's been an honor serving with you."

"**The next hit will bring down the shields, Captain,**" said Lucy. "**Your orders?**"

"On my command, self-destruct" ordered Jax. Lucy acknowledged.

In the viewscreen, the *Hellfire*'s crew could see one of the pirate ships making a run toward them that would end their lives. Jax was about to give his final order when the oncoming ship exploded into flames. Then the second ship exploded and the other three ships began to maneuver themselves to escape. They were not quick enough and they were destroyed by phaser fire coming from a vessel firing from the behind the *Hellfire*.

It was the *Fermi*. She had come out of warp directly above the *Hellfire* and her phaser banks unleashed a barrage that caught the pirates off guard.

Jax laughed and was about to yell when he caught himself. "Lucy, cancel self-destruct." Lucy acknowledged and Jax closed his eyes and concentrated. *'Captain, forget about us and help the Romulans.'* Seconds later the *Fermi* changed course and moved quickly toward the Romulan vessel.

As the *Fermi* moved away Jax said: "Now, that's what I call a dramatic entrance." Winters and Drid were jumping up and down together and whooping it up while Zitag'dur remained his usual stoic self.

"Okay gang, let's make it to Federation space. I'm sure there are Romulans converging on the area... Best possible speed."

On board the *Fermi*:

"Mister Orora, are all the torpedo bays loaded?"

"Yes, Captain, but our phasers are more than sufficient to disable those ships."

Annoyingly, the captain said, "I'm well aware of that but I want them to know that their days of terror have ended."

"Twenty seconds," said the *Fermi*'s helmsman, informing Capt. Aziz how much time was left before the ship dropped out of warp. Capt. Aziz acknowledged and turned to her security officer at the weapons station.

"Mister Orora, target and neutralize all ships with phaser fire except the ship containing the Poison Clan.' Lt. Orora acknowledged the order.

"I assume we plan on capturing those criminals" asked Cmdr. Montgomery?

The captain turned to him and simply said "Possibly." Cmdr. Montgomery stared at his captain and then looked at Cmdr. Gintok both wondering why someone who clearly states the reason she wants something done had become so evasive in the last few days.

Five, four, three, two, one. The *Fermi* dropped out of warp a little above and behind the *Hellfire*. It had a clear line of fire at the five pirate ships. The first phaser bolt hit the ship closest to the Clan's ship and completely destroyed it. The second ship's shields buckled under a sustained phaser blast and exploded seconds later.

The three other ships tried to evade the *Fermi* but they were no match for its maneuverability and weapons. Within a minute all five ships had been destroyed.

Cmdr. Montgomery looked at Capt. Aziz who appeared to be in a trance. "Mister Orora put a tractor beam on that pirate ship and we'll tow it back to Federation space."

Capt. Aziz' eyes opened. "Belay that order, Lieutenant. We'll deal with them later... Helmsman, take us into that fight."

Cmdr. Montgomery was incensed. "Captain. This is highly irregular. Please explain yourself?"

Capt. Aziz turned her head and stared at him. Immediately, he knew he had crossed into an area no officer should tread. He felt like hiding under his seat. After what seemed like an eon to him, she calmly said "I'll explain what I can later. Trust me." She turned her head back toward the viewscreen and began to form her next tactic.

There were still twenty ships left that were attacking the Romulan ship, although some appeared to be damaged. The scout ship had been taking a lot of punishment but it was still holding its own. It was only a matter of time until its shields failed and the pirates could either destroy it or attempt to board and capture it. Either way, taking down a Romulan military ship would greatly increase the pirates' fear factor that they held on numerous worlds.

As the *Fermi* approached, Saldor dispatched ten ships to intercept and engage it. The remaining ships would finish off the Romulans and reinforce the others. It was a good plan but they underestimated the *Fermi*'s captain.

As the pirate ships got within phaser range, the *Fermi* fired a volley of photon torpedoes into the attacking pirate ships, catching them totally off guard and obliterating three of the ships before they had gotten off a shot.

Because of the size of the pirate ships, using something as deadly as a photon torpedo would be considered overkill. It would also be considered a waste of resources on ships that small. Their shields could never withstand a direct hit from a photon torpedo and they knew it. The remaining ships were beginning to panic as they broke off their attack and headed for the safety of the Expanse. The *Fermi* took out two more fleeing ships with phaser fire and let the others run so it could assist the Romulan ship.

As the *Fermi* approached the scout ship, the classic 'fight or flight response' gripped the pirates. Four pirate ships turned to engage the *Fermi* while the other six decided it was best to withdraw. When the four noticed that their odds for survival had plummeted, they turned and raced for the Expanse.

As the first group of pirates approached the Expanse and safety, a Romulan Warbird suddenly uncloaked and began firing on them. The Warbird was five times the size of the *Fermi* and had enough firepower to destroy a planet. Anything within disruptor range would soon be destroyed.

With their escape route cut off by the Warbird, some of the pirates began to double back and try entering the Expanse at another point. That turned out to be a mistake because a second Romulan Scout Ship uncloaked and began firing on them. The pirates had lost two-thirds of their fleet in about twelve minutes. Seeing that the Romulans had things in hand, Capt. Aziz ordered the *Fermi* to pursue the *Hellfire*.

With no warp drive, the *Hellfire* had no chance of escaping.

"**Three minutes until the *Fermi* intercepts us,**" said Lucy.

"I guess that's our cue to head to the transporter pad," said Jax. He hailed Zitag'dur and Winters who were already down in the cargo hold and asked: "Are Zhak'San and our cuddly little friend all set to go?"

"Roger that, Captain," said Winters.

The transporter pad was in the *Hellfire*'s cargo bay so large objects could easily be moved around the cargo bay once they had beamed in.

Now for the final act.

As the *Fermi* approached, the *Hellfire* came about and began to attack, catching the *Fermi*'s crew off guard.

"What are they doing" asked Cmdr. Gintok? "They have no chance against us."

Capt. Aziz' eyes were closed while Cmdr. Gintok spoke and missed what he said. When she opened her eyes she said: "Mister Orora, lock on that ship and prepare to fire on my order."

Lt. Orora turned to her. "But Captain, they hardly have shields. A direct hit will destroy the ship."

"I'm aware of that, Mister. Do as you're ordered."

"Aye, Captain" he replied. Then the lieutenant turned around and seconds later said "Target locked. Awaiting your order."

Capt. Aziz closed her eyes again. Eight seconds later she opened them. "Fire." The forward phaser bank sent a bolt of energy toward the *Hellfire* and it exploded. Seconds later, there was no sign of any object ever being there.

The officers on the bridge stared at the viewscreen and then turned their attention toward Capt. Aziz who had a smile on her face.

"Captain," said Cmdr. Montgomery. "I seriously doubt if Starfleet will be entirely pleased with your actions today."

"The day is not over yet" replied the captain.

There was an audible pulse on the weapons console. Lt. Orora turned to look at it. He hesitated, then said "Captain, there are six objects just outside our port shields. It looks like five humanoid in environmental suits and someone in a stasis chamber."

"Beam them to Holodeck One and put guards on the outside."

"Holodeck One," asked Cmdr. Montgomery? "But these are..."

Capt. Aziz angrily turned her head toward him. "I believe I had asked you to trust me."

Cmdr. Montgomery stepped back and dropped his head. "You did, Captain. My apologies."

She turned to Lt. Orora. "Lieutenant, status?"

"The pirates have been beamed into Holodeck One. There appear to be two humans..."

"Lieutenant, neither you nor anyone else is authorized to scan the individuals who were just beamed aboard."

"Understood, Captain."

She rose from the captain's chair and said: "No one is allowed on or off this bridge until I return." She walked toward the door but stopped and turned around before leaving. "Commander" looking at Cmdr. Montgomery. "Pursue and capture any fleeing pirate ships." She turned and left the bridge.

Cmdr. Montgomery sat in the captain's chair. "You heard the captain. Scan for pirates."

Cmdr. Gintok walked over to him. "What just happened?"

"Some type of extraction. But who and for what purpose is anyone's guess." He chuckled. "This is going to be one of those days that you'll be telling your grandchildren about years from now."

Lt. Orora interrupted. "Commander. I'm picking up one ship traveling at warp six heading toward Federation space."

"Helmsman set a course to intercept."

When Capt. Aziz reached Holodeck One two heavily-armed guards were waiting by the entrance. They came to attention when she reached them and moved at her command. "No one is to enter or leave without my expressed permission." They acknowledged her. She took a deep breath, the doors slid open and she walked in.

The Emergency Medical Program was running on the holodeck when Capt. Aziz entered the room. She observed that Lt. Nandi and what looked like a Jem'Hadar had just removed what looked like a Romulan male from a stasis chamber and were moving him over to an operating table where the ship's Emergency Medical Physician was ready to operate.

There were also two others wearing environmental suits standing near the operating table with their backs to her, one tall and the other much shorter. The taller one was struggling to remove his helmet while the shorter one had his or her (she couldn't tell) helmet off and appeared to be a Ferengi.

Who are these people in my holodeck? Are they part of this program?

Without notice, the Ferengi spun around and pointed a pulse rifle at the captain's chest. The captain froze knowing that she was in no position to do anything but stand still. Holding the rifle was a Ferengi female. She appeared to be fairly old. Much older than one would expect for a mission like this.

The Ferengi's movement caught Lt. Nandi's eye and he focused in on the captain. "I would appreciate it if you wouldn't shoot my captain," said Lt. Nandi. "She may take it personally and take it out on me."

The Ferengi relaxed and lowered her weapon. "Sorry, Captain. It's been a trying day."

Capt. Aziz couldn't help but smile. "Yes, it has... for all of us." The Ferengi smiled.

The taller of the two finally removed his helmet. It was Petty Officer Winters. She smiled broadly. "Welcome aboard, Petty Officer."

"Thank you, Captain. It's good to be back" he replied with a smile.

"I take it you missed the advanced counter-terrorism program."

"I'm sure it was nice but the hands-on training I received was more educational."

I think Lieutenant Nandi is starting to have a bad influence on him.

She was about to step forward when she heard something moving to her left side. She looked to her side and saw nothing. She heard it again and looked down. She reflexively jumped to her right. On the floor was someone wearing an environmental suit struggling to get up. His hands were tied behind his back and his legs were bound. She stared down at him and then at Lt. Nandi.

"Oh, don't pay him any attention. He likes it down there" said Lt. Nandi as he stepped away from the operating table to let the doctor work.

She took one last look at whomever was on the floor and then began walking toward Lt. Nandi. She was about to say something to Lt. Nandi when she looked down on the operating table and saw a metal strip sticking out the side of the Romulan. She winced at the sight, then whispered a prayer for the Romulan's recovery.

Afterward, she looked at Jax and motioned to him that she needed to talk with him. He walked from around the operating table to meet her and both of them walked past Drid and Winters and stopped near the holodeck exit.

"So, how did it go" asked Capt. Aziz?

"To be succinct, Mission Accomplished" he replied without emotion. "Their base has been destroyed. Most of their ships were destroyed or damaged and you and the Romulans took care of their best crews... Some may have survived but without a base, they will be hunted down."

"And what about Krell?"

Lt. Nandi used his head to point to the person on the floor. "Want to say hello?"

They walked over to Krell. He struggled with his bindings. Lt. Nandi put his knee on Krell's chest to steady him and undid his helmet. Before it was completely off you could hear Krell snarling, hissing and cursing. "If you don't watch your language I'm going to put this helmet back on and seeing that your oxygen tank only has about 10 minutes of air left, things could get uncomfortable."

Krell snarled again but shut up when Lt. Nandi asked Winters to help him put on Krell's helmet.

"That's better," said Lt. Nandi. "Oh, where are my manners. I believe you two have met before but to refresh your memory this is Captain Aisha Aziz... The name might not be familiar but you are responsible for her standing over you today after she helped destroy your empire." Krell hissed and snarled. Lt. Nandi applied more knee pressure on Krell's chest and then rose.

Indeed the captain and Krell's paths had crossed. The captain was just a nineteen-year-old crewman on a cargo ship when Krell captured the ship and killed its captain in front of its crew. She and several other crewmembers were shackled and put on another ship so they could be sold as slaves, while the remaining crewmembers including her best friend, a Klingon woman named Malak, were left on board. Their bodies were later found on board except for Malak, whose body was never recovered. Fortunately, the pirates underestimated her abilities and made one mistake that allowed her to capture the ship and free her crewmembers.

After that, she was admitted into Starfleet Academy and although she wasn't one of the top students, she was one of the top leaders in her class. When she graduated from the Academy the Founders' War was taking place. Her leadership abilities and bravery enabled her to move through the ranks rapidly.

Now, here she was, standing over the most wanted criminal in the two quadrants whom she had sworn to bring to justice and suddenly realizing that he is the reason for her success. The irony of it sickened her. She wanted to smash her boot into his face repeatedly. He looked pathetic lying down there. His reign of terror had ended. He was finished. She walked away with her head hanging down.

Lt. Nandi asked Winters and Drid to replace his air tank and reattach his helmet. As they were doing it he looked down at Krell and said "Sorry, Your Magnificence, but we're tired of looking at you. So, you're going to have to stay in that getup until you're on a more secure vessel." Krell snarled and cursed. Lt. Nandi continued. "You better hope it's soon or else the inside of that suit is going to get pretty ripe."

Lt. Nandi walked over to Capt. Aziz. "Would you have preferred being a cook on a cargo ship?"

She mulled that question. "Maybe... Maybe I could have been a ship's captain one day."

"You are a ship's captain now and a damn good one."

She looked at Krell again and sighed. “How could you not want to kill him?”

“Who said I didn’t?” He took a deep breath. “If I had gone in alone. Krell would be dead and probably some of his lieutenants and that’s about all that would have happened… I would be dead and someone would have taken over the Brotherhood and they would be back doing what they’ve been doing.”

“But when I was given a team, I became responsible for their safety. We had to come up with a plan to do as much damage as we could and get out of there in one piece… Killing Krell became secondary.”

He glanced over at Krell struggling on the floor. “I’ve done far worse to him than death itself,” he said with a smile. “I think my wife and her team can be satisfied with that.”

She smiled, then looked over at Krell. “Now he can be brought to justice and pay for his crimes.”

Drid had her back to them but they could hear her laugh loudly. Startled by the laugh, Capt. Aziz looked at Lt. Nandi. “Why is she laughing?”

Lt. Nandi smiled. “Oh, there isn’t going to be a trial.” She looked surprised. He continued. “If you recall, the *Fermi* destroyed the ship with Krell and the Poison Clan on board. They’re dead. How can there be a trial if they’re dead?”

Capt. Aziz’ lower jaw dropped. “But why would you do that?”

He smiled. “In this business, it’s best to let everyone think you’re dead. That way they won’t come looking for you.”

She thought about it. “Okay. I understand that but what about Krell?”

“Oh, he can be useful at some point.”

“I don’t understand.”

“Okay. For example, a government has captured a valuable asset of yours that has a lot of information about you. You want that asset back alive and unharmed… Waving Krell in front of them as trade may make them want to talk to you.”

“The Federation would do that?”

"All governments do that. The bad thing about it in Krell's case is that we won't execute him but other governments will be more than happy to put him out of his misery."

The captain looked disgusted. "So he's a bargaining chip."

"Pretty much... But if it makes you feel any better, Krell might have some information that is extremely valuable to the Federation."

"And that is?"

"Sorry, that would be telling." She became irritated. "Oh, I forgot again." He turned toward Drid. "Captain, this is Drid. We have been a team for over thirty years." Both females exchanged pleasantries. There were a million questions the captain really wanted to ask her but now was not the time. "I hope we have the opportunity to sit down and have a thorough conversation one day."

"If you're ever on Vexia III stop by my bar. The drinks will be on the house."

The captain said she would even though she knew she probably wouldn't.

Lt. Nandi then directed her to the operating table where Zitag'dur was still assisting the holo-doctor in the operation.

"And this strapping young lad is Zitag'dur."

Zitag'dur nodded his head. "I have read your tactics at Torsett II. They were impressive for someone your age... The Dominion could have used someone of your skills."

She smiled. "Thanks but I was offered that job before and I turned it down. Things seemed to have worked out okay for me."

"They have indeed," said Zitag'dur bowing his head.

Lt. Nandi looked down at Zhak'San and said to the captain "I'd introduce him but we don't have a few days."

She studied his face. "Shouldn't he be in a real operating room with medical staff?"

"Normally I would agree with you but as far as this ship and Starfleet is concerned, he died with the rest of us a few minutes ago on the *Hellfire*."

Why does he make me out to be the bad guy in this?

"Look, I know this looks wrong to you and it probably is but you have to understand that this is the way business is transacted on this end of Starfleet. It's important that we stay anonymous. You can't do your job if people know who you are." He took a breath. "Right now, it's probably being reported to the Romulan High Command that the Poison Clan and Krell are dead. They're probably going to throw a party. But the Tal Shiar is going to think they've lost a really brave operative... If he dies on this table, they're going to be none the wiser. If he shows up in a few weeks, they're going to know the mission was successful and celebrate."

She shook her head. "So that's how it works?"

"Pretty much."

She was about to say something else but the ship shook. She tapped her communicator. "Aziz to bridge. What's our situation?"

"Captain, we've caught up to one of the remaining pirate ships. He doesn't want to surrender peacefully."

"I'm on my way." She looked at Lt. Nandi. "So, what's next?"

"Oh, I need you to contact Admiral Blaine. Just tell him 'The Poison Clan Rocks the World'. He'll know that the mission was accomplished and you've successfully extracted the strike team. He'll arrange a rendezvous point for the *Fermi* and a Starfleet Security vessel... It shouldn't take more than 36-48 hours. In the meantime, this will be our home. It would look kind of strange if Winters and I appeared out of nowhere."

She smiled. "Are you coming back?"

"Sure thing." He looked over at Winters. "Him too. We both like it here, don't we?"

Winters smiled. "It may be a little boring when we return but I think I can get used to it."

She turned to walk out the holodeck but Lt. Nandi said: "Oh, Captain, one last thing." She turned and looked at the lieutenant. "It would probably be a good idea if your bridge crew forgot about you beaming us on the ship and all." She stood there trying to process the request. "It will probably save you from having to answer a lot of uncomfortable questions."

That, she understood immediately. She smiled, turned and walked out of the holodeck.

Jax walked over toward the stasis chamber. He bent down and picked up a 3"x3"x3" cube and opened it up. There was a single toggle switch on the inside that he pressed to the 'On' position. Lights began to flash on the outside of the cube and after a few seconds, parts of the holoprogram began to flicker. Jax smiled and said, "Okay, sweetheart, tell me what you last remember?"

The voice of Lucy said: "**I have successfully interfaced with the ship's computer. I am scanning all ship's logs to update my records from when I was placed in the cube on the *Hellfire* and you reactivating me 12.61 seconds ago**."

"Nice to see you are alive and well," said Jax.

"**It is good that all of us made it**.'

"Well, not all of us," said Jax thinking about the loss of Neer.

He snapped out of it and walked over to the holo-doctor. "How's he doing?"

"**The surgery was a success but he's lost a lot of blood and needs a transfusion. I will have to synthesize some blood which will take time because of his unique blood type... I estimate it will take five-point-six hours to complete the synthesis**."

Jax shook his head. "No. The best thing to do is to just put him back into the stasis chamber and thaw him out when we get on board the other ship. Then we won't have to worry about who sees what." He paused. "Oh, Doctor, what were you saying a few seconds ago? I need you to do something for me."

Chapter 27

Capt. Aziz returned to the bridge just as the *Fermi* had neutralized the pirates' phasers and shields and was locking a tractor beam on their ship. Cmdr. Montgomery began to rise from the captain's chair to let her sit but she motioned him to stay seated while the operation was taking place.

Even though the tractor beam was secure the ship continued to resist, putting extreme stress on its engines.

"If she keeps that up, she'll explode," said Cmdr. Montgomery.

"These are desperate men, Commander. And desperate men do desperate things" replied the captain.

"Don't they know we won't kill or torture them?" asked Cmdr. Gintok.

"They're probably wanted in so many sectors that they think that whoever captures them will treat them as badly as they have treated others."

"Captain," said Lt. Cmdr. Anauk, the ship's science officer. "The ship's engines will explode shortly if they do not shut them down imm..."

She couldn't finish the sentence. One of the pirate ship's engines exploded which caused the other to explode and the ship disintegrated within the tractor beam.

The bridge crew was stunned. They just gawked at the viewscreen for the next minute. Then Capt. Aziz said, "I guess that was preferable to imprisonment."

She then walked in front of the viewscreen and faced her crew. "Can I have your attention?" Everyone focused on her. "By order of Starfleet Security, no one is to mention to anyone what transpired after the ship containing the criminals known as the Poison Clan was destroyed. The official Starfleet record of this incident is that there were no survivors... Do I make myself clear?" The crew nodded their assent.

"Good… And thank you for your patience with me. I will try to keep you better informed in the future… Helmsman set a course for the coordinates we used earlier today."

Cmdr. Montgomery rose again as she walked toward him but the captain motioned him to stay seated and said: "I'll be in my ready room."

Cmdr. Gintok walked over to Cmdr. Montgomery. "I'm not asking but do you have an opinion."

"I'm not giving you an opinion but something really big happened in the Expanse. Too bad we'll never know what it was."

Capt. Aziz sent two subspace transmissions that day. The first was to Adm. Blaine whom she informed of Lt. Nandi's message. The admiral thanked her for successfully extracting the Poison Clan and aiding in the destruction of the Talesian Brotherhood.

The second transmission was to Adm. Merino, Capt. Aziz' commanding officer. She told the admiral that she would debrief her as soon as possible but apologized in advance because some details in her story would be deemed classified by Starfleet Security.

She hated that part of this whole operation where she had to withhold information from her commanding officer and her crew. That was not part of her nature. She began to wonder if being a cook would have been preferable.

When the *Fermi* reached the Expanse the three Romulan ships were still there. The area was littered with the debris of pirate ships. It seemed that self-destructing their ships was preferable to surrender. She didn't blame them in this case because the Romulans were well known for their enhanced interrogation methods.

There was a brief conversation between Capt. Aziz and the commander of the damaged Romulan scout ship, whom she assumed was a member of the Tal Shiar. She was informed that two pirate ships had made it back into the Expanse. She wanted to tell the Romulans that they had nowhere to hide in the Expanse. As Lt. Nandi would probably say, 'That would be telling.' She would later inform Lt. Nandi of the escaped ships, who would express his hope that Saldor was not one of them. *'As a leader, he was more impressive than Krell.'*

The Romulan commander also expressed his thanks for her coming to the scout ship's aid and his regrets that the ship carrying Krell and the Poison Clan had been destroyed. "It is unfortunate that you had to destroy their ship but history has shown that the Poison Clan has a habit of resurrecting themselves even after their apparent deaths."

"That may be true," replied Capt. Aziz "but maybe we can use their current deaths to help improve relations between our two governments."

"Only time will tell, Captain."

After the conversation had ended, Capt. Aziz was left with the impression that the Romulan commander knew that everyone had survived the ship's destruction. *Maybe most extractions end with a ship being conveniently destroyed* she thought. Lieutenant Nandi had implied as much.

Three Federation starships were being dispatched to the area to search for survivors from Talese who would start making their way out of the Expanse to look for another safe haven. The first ship was to rendezvous with the *Fermi* in four hours. After that, there was no reason to stay at the Expanse and the *Fermi* could begin its trip back to the Ostara system to watch the sun nova before it began its collapse.

Shortly after they departed the Expanse, Adm. Blaine provided the *Fermi* with the rendezvous coordinates of the Starfleet Security vessel. The rendezvous would take place in eighteen hours. It was a relief knowing that the Poison Clan was leaving and that the *Fermi* would get back to normal although dealing with scientists on a daily basis skewed the definition of normal.

Three hours later word went out that the Talesian Brotherhood suffered a fatal blow when the *USS Fermi* along with three Romulan vessels defeated a large force of Brotherhood ships. Reports confirm that Kradik Krell, the Brotherhood's leader, and the notorious gang called the Poison Clan were killed during this action.

Capt. Aziz and her crew had become heroes. This embarrassed her. Not for what she actually did, which in itself was extraordinary, but for what the Poison Clan accomplished and would never receive credit for it.

Fifteen hours later the *Fermi* rendezvoused with a Starfleet Security starship whose registry number and captain's name did not appear in the Starfleet database. As the ship went into warp after the transfer had completed Capt. Aziz shook her head. *It's a strange group of people who make up Section 31. It's amazing that they seem to have no trouble finding people to do this kind of work.*

Chapter 28

The *Fermi* returned to the Ostara system 36 hours before the expected nova. There was time to gather her scientists who by now were grumbling loudly about being moved around like the children of divorced parents. Many of them vowed that they would complain to the Federation Science Council about the way they were being treated. Most of them had been so preoccupied that they had not even heard about the *Fermi*'s exploits at the Typhon Expanse. Some had but brushed it aside because the nova was of far more importance. Such is the life of a starship captain.

Then it happened. The sun's core collapsed so fast that sensors surrounding the sun didn't have time to inform the scientists that it had taken place. In approximately 2.3 hours the shock waves from the core collapse would reach the surface of the sun making it brighten. The sun would continue to brighten for the next three to four months expelling half its mass during the process and becoming a white dwarf star. During the next several years the sun would cool and eventual be the temperature of its surroundings.

The *Fermi* was only scheduled to stay in Ostara system one more week before it was to depart and go to its next assignment. Prior to that, the *Fermi* had to make a stop at Starbase 205 where Capt. Aziz would be debriefed by Adm. Merino and several other ranking officers. She was not looking forward to this because there were questions that she would refuse to lie about and ones that she would have to refuse to answer. It was a horrible situation for her to be in.

Two days prior to the debriefing Capt. Aziz contacted Adm. Blaine to let him know that she was going to be candid and would only refuse to divulge the names of the Poison Clan personnel. The admiral thanked her for her honesty and said that he would contact Adm. Merino in the hopes that she would make her debriefing as painless as possible. Capt. Aziz thanked him but wasn't sure what he could do.

It wasn't painless but it could have been a lot worse. The night before the meeting, Adm. Merino received a classified document from Adm. Blaine explaining Capt. Aziz' role in retrieving a group of Starfleet Security operatives who were on a mission to infiltrate the Talesian Brotherhood, capture or kill its leader, Kradik Krell, and destroy as much of their infrastructure as possible. Starfleet Security also instructed Adm. Merino to only allow other members of the debriefing panel access to the document providing they possessed the necessary security clearances. Both Fleet Captains Thon Zitune and Unya Tun possessed that clearance and were able to review the documents. Ironically, the only person without access was Capt. Aziz. Needless to say, she was a bit aghast when she realized that she may never know what happened inside the Typhon Expanse. But what really irked her was that neither Lt. Nandi nor PO Winters could ever tell her what had happened unless she reached that security level and Adm. Blaine gave express permission for her to know about it.

What did gave her great pleasure was when she was asked about when and how she was able to communicate with the operatives. "I'm really sorry but that information is classified" she replied trying not to smile.

Now knowing what the extent of the operation had been, Adm. Merino recommended that a commendation be given to the crew of the *Fermi* for their bravery and initiative. The fact that Section 31's role in this action was swept under the carpet annoyed Captain Aziz to a great degree. As far as Starfleet line officers were concerned Section 31 was like a bogeyman spreading mischief throughout the service. Capt. Aziz had learned that this assessment was far from the truth.

Chapter 29

One week later, the *Fermi* rendezvoused with the *USS Eroica* which was heading to Starbase 205 to rotate some of its personnel. The *Eroica* was also bringing back one of the *Fermi*'s best engineers.

The transporter beam energized and two figures materialized. One was Lt. Jackson Nandi and the second was his Bajoran cat, Crewman Kaso.

“Greetings Lieutenant. How was your shore leave?” asked the transporter chief.

“Oh, nowhere near as exciting as yours,” replied Jax. “You guys were really busy with wiping out pirates and watching stars die.” He lifted his hands in exasperation. “I always seem to miss all the action.”

“Well, you did have a good reason for not being here.”

Jax shrugged. “Yeah, unfortunately, I did.” He shrugged again. “Oh, well, back to work.” He looked down at his cat. “Okay, Crewman, let’s go find our new quarters.”

Jax waved to the transporter chief and left the transporter room. From there he took a turbolift to the deck where the officers’ quarters were and began looking for his new home. Purely by coincidence, Capt. Aziz came out of her apartment and began walking toward the turbolift. She hesitated when she saw him but then smiled and continued walking. Lt. Nandi smiled and stopped.

“Captain.”

“Lieutenant. How as your shore leave?”

“Very good, Captain. I actually got to see the nova on a holoprojector in a bar on Vexia III. It’s not as good as being there but the crowd was fun and you could drink Romulan Ale.”

“Isn’t Romulan Ale illegal?”

“Not on Vexia III.” He hesitated and changed the subject. “I take it Petty Officer Winters is back?”

"Yes. He returned two days ago." She was beginning to hate this game of pretending nothing happened but both of them had their orders.

"You know, not that I have any say in the matter but I think that Petty Officer Winters would make an excellent Chief someday." Capt. Aziz looked at him inquisitively. He finished by saying "Seeing that he completed all these special training courses and all."

She wanted to laugh but couldn't. "Maybe someday he will."

"Well, if you will excuse me, the Crewman and I have to find our new home. And I'm sure you have more important things to do than talk to me."

He turned to leave but Capt. Aziz abruptly said "Lieutenant?" He turned to face her and she asked: "Why are you here?"

He gave her a feigned look of shock. "Because I work here... Or I did unless I've been transferred."

She became irritated. "This has nothing to do with recent events. I am the captain of this ship and I demand to know why Admiral Blaine has you on this ship."

His face turned serious. "My apologies Captain but that would be telling."

Her blood pressure spiked. She was about to say something but realized that she had just been put in a position where she had to withhold information from her superiors because of the sensitivity of it. She calmed herself and simply said "Very good, Lieutenant. That will be all."

He smiled and nodded as he said "Captain." Then turned and walked away with his cat.

As he walked down the corridor she couldn't stop wondering why this man had initially been put on her ship and why it was so important that he stay. She mulled numerous possibilities but none made logical sense. She would have pondered it longer but she realized that she had other duties to perform. She turned and walked into the turbolift which would take her to the bridge where she would start another day as captain of the *USS Fermi*.

Epilogue

Since their first encounter with the alien race in the Tukaris system one year ago, the Romulan Empire has engaged its new enemy with increased frequency. The enemy whose tactic of sending a large mother-ship along with two smaller, heavily-armed escorts when they encroach Romulan Space has caused them to reallocate ships and resources from other parts of the Empire to reinforce their existing forces. In spite of this increase in ships, the best the Romulans have done would be considered a stalemate.

Six weeks ago, alien soldiers were able to land and secure a small planetoid in Romulan space. Within four days the Romulan fleet was of sufficient numbers where they were able to destroy or force the withdrawal of all the enemy vessels.

With air superiority and an enemy who could not be reinforced or resupplied the Romulans landed 25,000 troops to attack the estimated 10,000 enemy troops. Within two days the enemy had killed over 6,000 Romulan soldiers and wounded over 8,000. 20,000 more troops were put into the battle and as of this day, the Romulans have not secured the planet.

When word of the battle reached Romulus, the Imperial Senate was livid. Even the Jem'Hadar had succumbed to the Romulans when they held the advantage. How was it then possible for an opponent to inflict so many casualties in so short a time and still continue to fight? It troubled them that they had put so many resources into the battle and so far all they had gotten out of it was a draw. At what point would the Empire have to move most of their military on one stretch of border to defend against one enemy? At some point, they would have to either decisively defeat their enemy, whom they still knew little about, or they would need help in doing it.

The Empire, in general, eschewed asking for help from any outside source. They were a proud race and distrustful of everyone. Seeking help would be a sign of weakness. But it was becoming apparent that if the enemy were to launch an offensive on multiple fronts their military may be stretched too thin.

Even if they needed help, who would help them? Definitely not the Klingons who would celebrate the defeat of the Empire and probably not the Federation whom they had not had formal relations with in over two years.

But then the Imperial Senate learned from a high-ranking Tal Shiar officer that several months ago Starfleet Security had asked for the Tal Shiar's help in aiding a Federation team to infiltrate the Talesian Brotherhood's base in the Typhon Expanse to catch or kill its leader and destroy its infrastructure. The Tal Shiar agreed and sent in an operative of their own to assist them.

A Tal Shiar ship engaged a fleet of pirate ships that were trying to prevent the operatives from escaping and came under heavy fire. The ship would have been destroyed if it weren't for the help of a Federation starship captained by a human woman name Aisha Aziz who deployed tactics that could best be said to be unconventional.

The Senate wondered why this particular human was of such interest to the Tal Shiar. That was when the Tal Shiar officer produced a classified document reporting the uncensored events that took place during the Dominion War at Torsett II.

After reading the document, one of the ranking senators said: "I believe it is time for us to meet this Captain Aziz."

***** End Book One *****

Made in the USA
San Bernardino, CA
12 May 2020

71380458R00115